# Shadows At Jamestown

By Steven K. Smith

MyBoys3 Press

*To Josh,*
*and your late-night writing sessions*

# SHADOWS AT JAMESTOWN

# PROLOGUE

The paddle of the canoe was the only sound in the thick night air, barely audible as it slipped in and out of the water. Drifting steadily, like a shadow across the calm of the river, it blended with the darkness.

As the canoe neared the island, a shadow hopped into the knee-deep water, tugging the small craft ashore and into the clearing hidden among the tall reeds. Once the craft was secured, the figure reached into the canoe, lifting out a small duffel bag. Crouching, the figure scanned the trees for movement, then glanced back at the black waters of the James River to ensure no one had followed.

The faint call of a whip-poor-will rang out from the trees. The untrained ear would have dismissed it as a common noise in the night, but the silent visitor knew it was much too late for a songbird's call. A figure emerged from the tree line, advancing toward the undergrowth that still hid the first shadowy figure.

Neither shadow spoke, they only traded simple nods. The person from the woods exchanged a wooden box for the duffel bag, completing their transaction. Both people knew the small box contained a relic of incalculable value, while the duffel contained bundles of money whose value was quite measurable. In fact, the dollars had been accumulating nicely in a hidden bank account for the past several months since the secret smuggling ring had begun.

A handshake took place before the first shadow silently returned to the river and the canoe. The figure from the trees remained, a moment longer than needed, watching the moon emerge from the clouds to cast a pale glow across the water. The figure considered how the river could have looked quite similar hundreds of years ago, in the times when the First People lived alone near these waters, amongst the trees. They were dangerously unaware of the European settlers who would soon be crossing the great ocean. First in just a trickle, but then as a great flood. The settlers would nearly wipe out everything that was once precious to the people known as the Powhatan.

The buzz of a cell phone interrupted the historical musings, pulling the figure's thoughts back to the current century. It was a reminder to keep moving or there would be questions, and questions would lead to problems. The recent discovery of the West Wall was a monumental event. As one of the earliest remnants of the first Jamestown settlers from four hundred years ago, it was making news around the world. Everyone had an interest, and interest meant money.

A lot of money.

# CHAPTER ONE

"I can't just leave you here like this," Mom said, her voice a little shaky. "I didn't think I'd have to do this for at least a few more years. You boys are growing up too fast."

Sam stood awkwardly with his mom and his brother, Derek, in the grassy area in front of the dorms at the College of William & Mary in Williamsburg, Virginia. He and Derek and their friend Caitlin had been invited by Professor Evanshade to spend a week as part of a summer program at historic Jamestown.

And it wasn't just a regular summer camp like most kids their ages went to—this was called Field School. It was a program to assist with Jamestown's archaeological digs. Most of the other attendees were graduate students. Many came from the University of Virginia, but there were also people there from colleges all over the country.

The college students spent six weeks in Field School, but Caitlin, Derek, and Sam would only be here one week.

Professor Evanshade had called to invite all three of them to visit just as school was ending for the summer, knowing how they loved history. They'd met the professor on several past adventures when they had found lost coins in a mine, tracked a treasure from the American Revolution, and after an incident at the Civil War museum at Tredegar.

It was going to be awesome.

Derek shot Sam a look, and Sam knew his brother well enough to guess exactly what he was thinking. The sooner they could get Mom to leave, the better.

"C'mon, Mom," said Derek. "It's not like we're actually going to college. It's only a few days. We'll be fine."

Mom nodded and wiped an eye with a shaky hand.

He'd never let Derek see it, but Sam was feeling a little shaky too, or maybe he was just nervous. He'd never spent a week away from home before, and even though it would be fun, he was worried he'd miss his parents. One good thing had already come from this experience though. He'd finally been able to convince his parents to get him a cell phone. Derek had had one for nearly a year now, something he reminded Sam of at least three times a day. And Sam was now quick to point out that he'd gotten a cell phone at age eleven, while Derek hadn't gotten his until he was thirteen.

"You two are going to have so much fun," Mom said. "I have such great memories of this place from when I was in college. Did I tell you about the time we—"

"Yeah, you told us that story," Derek said. "We have to go find our dorm room, so now's a good time to say goodbye."

"I can help you unpack," Mom said.

That sounded like a good idea to Sam. He had no idea how to find their room or figure out where to meet Professor Evanshade.

"Mom," Derek groaned. "It's a boys' dorm. You really *don't* want to go in."

Mom sighed. "Okay. You two go and get settled. Then we'll go to Professor Evanshade's office."

Derek looked like he was in pain. "You don't have to do that. We'll find it."

"I'm not leaving until I deliver you to Professor Evanshade personally," said Mom. "Now go unpack. I'll wait here."

Sam followed Derek into the dorm building, struggling with his sleeping bag, pillow, and suitcase. As they trudged up the stairwell, sweat dripped from Sam's forehead.

"Come on, slowpoke!" urged Derek. "We're gonna spend all day on the stairs if you don't hurry."

Sam groaned and tried to ignore his older brother. He

wanted to get out of the staircase too—it had to be ninety degrees in the airless space.

They finally emerged from the stairwell onto the third floor. Derek found their dormitory room halfway down the hallway. "Here we are," he said, bursting into the room. "Home, sweet home."

"Just for a week," said Sam.

"Close enough," answered Derek. "It feels like we're in college though, doesn't it?"

"I guess," Sam answered, unrolling his sleeping bag onto the bottom bunk. He hadn't had to share a room with Derek for two glorious years, but it was a sacrifice he was willing to make if it meant coming to Field School. He put his clothes in a drawer and set a flashlight, a toiletries bag, a couple of books, and his phone on the dresser.

"Mom's waiting for us. We'd better hurry."

Derek stood in front of his dresser, combing his hair in the mirror on the wall. "Just a second—I want to make sure I look good for all the college ladies. I think they might dig the younger man type, don't you think?"

Sam rolled his eyes. "Give me a break." His brother was heading into eighth grade but usually acted like he thought he was going into college. If he were half as mature as he thought he was, life would be a lot better for everyone.

While Derek primped, Sam pulled back the curtain

and looked out the window at the campus. Williamsburg was only a short drive from Jamestown, so the participants of Field School stayed in dorms at the College of William & Mary. It was one of the oldest colleges in the country and sat right on top of Colonial Williamsburg, a place full of history and archeology in its own right. They'd visited Williamsburg before during an adventure at the Wythe House, where they had ended up chasing a bad guy named Jerry.

Sam wondered whether he'd prefer to go to a school in a quiet tree-covered setting like this or one in a bustling city. He wasn't sure, but he figured he had plenty of time to decide. Right now he was just glad to be on summer vacation and not yet starting sixth grade. Middle school seemed like a big change, and he wasn't looking forward to being one of the youngest kids at school again.

When Derek finally declared his hair perfect, the brothers went back outside. Even though it was summer, people were everywhere—college-age students, tourist groups, and families. It was one of those Virginia summer days that got hot early and stayed that way. Sam was pretty used to the warmer weather now, different as it was to when he lived up north. Most of the year was nice, but the mugginess sometimes still surprised him.

They found Mom, and someone was with her.

"Look who I found," said Mom.

"Hey, guys!" Caitlin waved at Derek and gave Sam a quick hug.

Derek snickered and Sam shot him a dirty look. He was always going on about Caitlin being Sam's girlfriend, but they were just good friends. She was a great investigator, and Sam thought she might be even more excited about this camp than he was.

"Isn't this amazing?" said Caitlin. "I can't wait to get over to the dig site."

"I know," Sam said. "Me too."

"Let's head to the car and I'll take you to over to Jamestown and the Field School," Mom said.

Derek pointed at the building behind Caitlin. "Is this where you're staying?"

"Yeah, it's nice."

"Do you have a roommate?" Derek asked, a sly grin on his face. Sam wanted to groan. Mom was ahead a few paces and hadn't heard.

Caitlin frowned. "No, they gave me a single, which at first I was sad about, but I guess it will be good to have my own space." She nudged Sam in the ribs with her elbow. "Besides, I have you guys to hang out with, right? So it shouldn't be too bad."

Sam nodded with a smile. Caitlin was an only child. She probably would have preferred a chance to meet more girls her age, but all the other people in Field School were college age or older. He couldn't imagine having to live with a stranger who was that much older than him. Sam had Derek, but he wasn't sure if that was lucky or not.

"I can't believe we're going to be working where the first settlers came to America," Caitlin gushed. "There's no place else like it in the whole country. Isn't it exciting?" She had been reading nonstop about the area's history and was already peppering Sam with facts.

"Isn't this where Pocahontas lived?" asked Derek, who'd barely done any research at all. He tended to jump into things first and figure them out later. Somehow he didn't mind looking clueless.

Caitlin frowned. "It's so much more than that, Derek. I love Pocahontas, but she was just a small part of the story. You'll see."

"Sure," replied Derek. "Captain Jack Sparrow and all that. I remember."

Sam shook his head. "Wrong movie, dummy."

"I think you mean Captain John Smith," said Caitlin.

Derek flashed a silly grin. "Right, I was just testing you."

They drove fifteen minutes down the road until they reached Jamestown, following signs for the historic section on the island. Caitlin barely stopped talking long enough to take a breath, or at least that's how it seemed to Sam. They pulled up to a building called the visitor center. The lady at the front desk directed them to Dr. Evanshade's office down the hallway.

"It should be right around here somewhere," Mom said, glancing up at the room numbers.

"Well, that's preposterous!" a voice yelled from inside one of the offices.

Sam thought he recognized the professor's voice.

"I'm getting sick and tired of these allegations," said the voice sternly. "There is no way that such a thing could have happened. Furthermore, who in their right mind would want to do such a thing?"

It was the professor, all right. But Sam had never heard him sound so cross before.

# CHAPTER TWO

"Oh, dear," Mom said, wincing. "I hope everything's okay. Maybe this is a bad time..."

"I'm sure it's fine," Derek said.

Sam took a step back from the door as the voice began again.

"I just don't understand it. There has to be some kind of mistake." Another pause, then, "Charlie, I'm going to have to call you back."

They heard the phone drop back on the cradle and a chair roll across the floor. Caitlin nodded and they stepped into the doorway. The professor looked preoccupied for a moment, but then he glanced up at them and his face changed to his regular, cheery smile. "Excellent!" he shouted as they entered the office. "It's my favorite young students."

"Hey, Professor!" said Derek.

Sam looked around the small office. The walls were covered with shelves holding hundreds of books, stacks of papers, and old-looking artifacts. It was a mess, but in an important-looking kind of way.

The older man walked over and shook their hands vigorously. His white beard was slightly longer than the last time Sam had seen him, but he still wore his large, round glasses that made his eyes look bigger than they really were.

"Sorry if we came at a bad time," said Caitlin.

"What?" said the professor, as if nothing had been wrong. "Oh, that's just some administrative nonsense." He paused as a slight twitch ran over his face, then smiled again. "It takes more of my time around here than I'd like, I'm afraid. Keeps me from being out in the field, discovering history."

"That's why we came!" said Caitlin energetically.

"I'm so glad you did," said the professor, building enthusiasm as he spoke. "You kids are going to have the time of your lives. And what a week! Why, I can hardly contain myself about the West Wall. Just imagine what could be out there for us to find."

"Well," said Mom. "I suppose it's time for me to make my exit."

Derek widened his eyes as if to say it was about time. She hugged both Sam and Derek quickly and headed for the doorway.

"Bye, Mom," said Sam.

"Keep an eye on these two for me," she whispered to Caitlin on her way out.

Caitlin nodded with a smile.

Mom hurried out, as if she wanted to leave before she changed her mind.

Derek let out a sigh of relief.

Right after Mom left, two college-age students, a boy and a girl, walked into the professor's office. Both were dressed in T-shirts, shorts with lots of pockets, and hiking boots. They looked ready to trek the Appalachian Trail. The guy's T-shirt had a picture of a bone and read "*I found this humerus.*" Sam was pretty sure that was a joke.

"Ah, perfect timing," the professor said. "Toby and Grace, let me introduce you to our youngest team members. They're top-notch discoverers, these three. Show them around Jamestown, won't you? I've got a couple of important phone calls to make. Then I'll join you for lunch."

"Sure thing, Doc," said Grace. "Come on, guys. We'll take the Jeep."

"Finally!" whispered Derek as they filed out of the office.

On their way out, the professor was already on the phone again. "Listen, I'm going to need to see those test results."

Sam noticed Toby and Grace pause and glance nervously

at each other. He wondered if they knew what the professor had been arguing about. Once everyone was in the hallway, Toby reached back and pulled the professor's door shut.

Derek stepped forward, brushing his hair back and shaking Grace's hand. "Hey, you know all that stuff he said about top-notch discoverers? He's mostly talking about me. I'm Derek."

Sam rolled his eyes and coughed.

"Oh, right, and this is my kid brother, Sam, and this is Caitlin. They help out sometimes too."

"Help out—?" Sam started to object.

"Ignore Derek," said Caitlin. "He's deluded. Are you both in college? Have you been here for the whole summer?"

Grace nodded. "We are, and it's been great. I'm a double major at the University of Virginia."

Sam frowned. "What's a double major?"

"It's when you focus on two different fields of study, right?" said Caitlin, showing off.

"Exactly," said Grace. "Mine are Anthropology and Medieval Art."

That sounded like a lot of work to Sam. It was probably perfect for Caitlin.

"And I came from the University of Pennsylvania, focusing on Early American Studies," said Toby. "But Grace is right, it's been a fantastic few weeks. You've heard about the West Wall discovery, I'm sure. It's already been full of treasures."

"That sounds incredible." Caitlin was almost trembling with enthusiasm.

"Well then let's go," said Toby. "You're going to love it. But first we'll drive you on a loop to give you a feel for where things are."

Sam had read in the newspaper about the West Wall, a brand-new section of the colonial site that had recently been discovered. It was part of the reason he was so excited to be here when they were. He took a deep breath as he followed Grace and Toby, his mind racing over what new treasures they might find.

Toby drove the Jeep off the island across a thin stretch of land surrounded on both sides by water. The area to the left was swampy, but to their right was a huge body of water. Sam didn't think they were that close to the ocean. "Is that the bay?"

"No, that's the James River," answered Grace. "It's where the Jamestown settlers sailed inland when they reached the Chesapeake Bay. Named after King James himself."

"Wow," said Sam. "It's so much wider than the part that runs through Richmond. It's hard to believe it's the same river." He thought about the journeys they'd had across the river by Belle Isle and Hollywood Cemetery.

While he didn't spot any rapids like they'd seen there, this part must be ten times as wide across.

Further down the road, Grace pointed out the window to a large parking lot with a row of flags flying in the center. "This is the Jamestown Settlement. It's a welcome center and museum that tells all about the first settlers here at Jamestown. There's a recreation of an Indian village, the fort, and even the ships."

"Is that where we'll be working?" asked Sam, staring out the window. The large building behind the parking lot didn't look much like an early settler's fort.

Toby turned and smiled. "Nah, that part is for tourists. There's no actual archeology going on there."

"That's right," said Grace. "The actual land where the Jamestown colonists lived is back on the island. That's where all the excavation is happening and where Doc's discoveries have been made."

"Doc?" asked Sam.

"Oh, sorry. Professor Evanshade," replied Grace. "Most of us on the dig site just call him Doc."

"Cool," said Derek.

"I can't wait to see it," exclaimed Caitlin. "I hope we actually get to find something."

Grace laughed. "Oh, I'm sure you will. It seems like almost every day we find something new, especially since the West Wall discovery."

"This is a great week to be here," added Toby. "You three are lucky."

Derek grinned. "Nah, we just have perfect timing."

On their way back to the island, Sam noticed a sign pointing to a small building in a wooded area on their right. "Glasshouse," he read.

"Did they build a house out of glass?" asked Derek.

Toby and Grace laughed. Somehow they seemed to think Derek was funny. "No, that's where the glass-blowers worked."

"They blew glass?" asked Sam. He'd never heard of that before.

"Where do you think glass comes from?" said Caitlin.

Sam's mind went blank. He honestly had no idea where glass came from, besides the store.

"We'll show it to you later," said Toby. "It's pretty fascinating."

Sam guessed that a lot of modern things he took for granted weren't quite as easy to make back then. He'd probably learn more this week than he'd even imagined.

Toby drove down a service road behind the visitor center toward another building that looked like a house. "Here we are," he said as they pulled up to a smaller building.

"This is the dig site?" asked Caitlin.

Grace nodded. "This is the science building. The

historic area and the Archaearium are behind it, closer to the water."

"Archaearium?" asked Caitlin.

Sam chuckled quietly. Caitlin thought she knew everything, and it was always fun to see her stumped.

"It's the museum that shows all the artifacts that have been found in the historic area," explained Grace. "There are nearly four thousand of them."

"Wow," said Sam. Maybe they really would find something. "They're probably pretty valuable, huh?"

Grace grinned. "Let's just say it would only take a couple of them to pay off my college loans."

Sam wasn't exactly sure how college loans worked, but he knew college was expensive. That's why he and Derek were planning to get baseball scholarships.

They walked through a side door into a small workroom with lockers on the wall. "This is where we store our stuff," said Toby, leading them through the hall. "Down there's the lab and some meeting rooms. But there's one place that you want to be sure to remember how to find."

"Sounds important," said Caitlin.

"Oh, it is." Grace nodded.

"The dig site?" asked Sam.

"Not quite," Toby said. "The café. It's almost lunchtime!"

# CHAPTER THREE

S am and Caitlin found two open chairs at a long
table. Derek sat next to Grace, and Toby took a seat
between two other people. Box lunches waited in front of
each of them. Sam was hungrier than he'd thought, but
no one was eating yet, so he tried not to think about his
empty stomach.

While they waited for the professor to join them, the
others introduced themselves. Two were visiting profes-
sors, three were college students, one was an archeologist
named Patrick, and the laboratory scientist was named
Marcus. Sam felt pretty out of place among all the knowledge and experience in the room, but he reminded
himself it would be a great place to learn.

The professor came rushing in and apologized for
keeping everyone waiting. "Go ahead, dig in, everybody!"

Sam unpacked a turkey sandwich, an apple, and bottled water.

Caitlin had already taken a bite of her sandwich. "It's good."

Sam leaned closer to Caitlin. "What do you think those phone calls were about?" he asked under his breath.

"You mean the professor?"

"Yeah, I've never seen him upset like that."

She nodded. "I don't know, but Toby and Grace seemed worried."

"I thought so too."

Before Sam could consider things any further, the professor walked to the head of the table. "I know most of you have already heard this, but since we have new team members this week, I thought it would make sense to share some information about our little operation here with them." He placed his laptop on the table next to a black cable. "Toby, could you help me with this?"

"Sure, Doc." Toby connected the cable to the professor's laptop, and an image filled the flat-screen monitor on the wall behind them.

"Who can tell me what this is?" asked the professor.

Sam studied the image. It was clearly a map. He could pick out the difference between rivers and other bodies of water from the land. It was somewhere along the coast, but he couldn't quite place it.

"It's Virginia, right?" asked Derek.

"Not the Virginia I know," said Caitlin. "What happened to Maryland above it?"

The professor chuckled. "Well, it's turned sideways from how we're used to looking at things, but it's surprisingly accurate. This was one of the first maps of Virginia, drawn by none other than John Smith."

"Captain John Smith?" asked Sam.

"The very one," answered the professor. "Just over four hundred years ago, in 1606, one hundred and four brave and industrious men and boys headed out from London, England seeking a new life. Led by Captain Christopher Newport, it took them six months to cross the Atlantic. Eventually, after brief stops in the Canary Islands and the West Indies, they reached the mouth of the Chesapeake Bay. They headed sixty miles up the James River to where we're meeting right now, what we know as Jamestown."

"Right," said Derek. "On the Mayflower. We know all about this."

Grace laughed. "Wrong. The Mayflower landed in Plymouth, Massachusetts, not Virginia. And that was nearly fifteen years later. John Smith was one of the colonists who came with Captain Newport on that early voyage to Jamestown."

"Very true," said the professor. "After all those months at sea, the group settled on this stretch of land due to its deep water port and secure vantage point in the river which allowed them to see any potential attackers."

"Unfortunately for them," added Toby, "it didn't work out as well as they'd hoped at first. They were quickly attacked by the Powhatan Indians, and many of the settlers perished during the first winter."

"Gosh, that's terrible," said Sam. He'd never really thought about how hard it might have been to sail across the ocean for such a long time only to reach the new land and die.

"We've uncovered a great deal in recent years that helps us understand their situation," said the professor. "Most of it is rather unpleasant, I'm afraid. Despite successfully building the fort, the settlers' second winter in Jamestown is known as the Starving Time."

"They died of starvation?" asked Sam.

"Many of them," said Toby. "In fact, we recently discovered some remains that prove there were periods when the settlers resorted to cannibalism."

"Cannibalism!" exclaimed Derek. "You mean, like, eating people?"

The professor nodded solemnly. "That's right."

"Who did they eat?" asked Sam, slowly. "The Native Americans?"

"No," said Grace. "The Indian tribes, that's actually what we call them in Virginia, not Native Americans, were quite advanced and resourceful. You might also call

them the First People, or First Nation. But the cannibalism Toby's talking about was between the settlers.
They likely ate some of their own."

"Oh," gasped Caitlin, her face turning pale. "That's
awful."

The turkey Sam was chewing suddenly lost its appeal.
He put the rest of his sandwich back in the box.

"Very," said Grace. "But thankfully, a small band of
sixty made it through the winter. Even so, things were so
bad they were ready to abandon the colony. In fact, they
were literally sailing up the river to return to England
when they met a desperately needed reinforcement ship
with more colonists, food, and supplies."

"Just in the nick of time," said Derek.

"For some, at least," said the professor. "Too late for
many, I'm afraid."

"I wonder what would have happened if they hadn't
met that ship," said Caitlin.

"History is filled with many such 'what ifs,'" said the
professor.

"Maybe Jamestown would have been abandoned alto-
gether," said Sam. He thought about the stories he'd
heard about the Lost Colony on Roanoke Island. Maybe
Jamestown only narrowly avoided disappearing as well.

"Fortunately for us, we'll never know." The professor
glanced at the clock on the wall. "You'll learn more about
all that soon enough. I could sit here talking about this all

day, but you came here to see history for yourself and to get your hands dirty. Would you like to visit the dig?"

"Sweet," said Sam, wadding up his napkin.

The professor smiled. "Toby and Grace will be serving as your mentors for the week. Of course I'll be in and out as well, and you're welcome to ask the rest of the team any questions you may have."

"When do we get started?" asked Caitlin.

"How about right now?" said Grace, pushing back her chair. "Most of the team is already out there."

"Let's go!" Derek said with a grin.

"We'll stop by the break room," said Toby. "Each of you will have a pack with some of the basic tools you'll need for the week. Then we're going to head over to the West Wall. Might as well get you right to the heart of the action."

Sam grinned. He wondered what they might unearth. Could they really make a monumental discovery even though they were just kids there for the week? It seemed unlikely, but the way the others were talking, it was like fishing from a barrel, as their neighbor Mr. Haskins often said. Sam stood up and headed for the door, his mind filled with anticipation.

# CHAPTER FOUR

A paved pathway cut through some marsh toward the river. Even in the daytime, the frogs and bugs were making a racket. Enormous red dragonflies circled the swamp, dive-bombing the tourists, their double sets of wings looking like biplanes. Sam noticed a tall monument poking out from behind the trees. It was made of concrete and had to be at least fifty feet high. It reminded him of the Washington Monument in Washington, DC.

"What is that?" asked Caitlin.

"It commemorates the three-hundredth anniversary of the founding of Jamestown," answered Grace.

"Didn't the professor just tell us Jamestown was four hundred years old, not three hundred?" said Sam.

Grace smiled. "It is, but this monument was built here over a hundred years ago."

"Wow," marveled Derek. "Even the monuments about history are historic around here."

Toby chuckled. "You'd better get used to it. Outside of the Indian settlements, which were, of course, the original settlements on this land, Jamestown is about as old as it gets here in America." As they walked forward, Toby pointed out different buildings. "Over there is the Archaearium."

"That's what you were telling us about in the car," said Caitlin. "Where the artifacts are."

Toby nodded. "And up here is the church and the fort. Further over is the West Wall. That's where we're headed."

As they approached a red brick church, Caitlin stopped at a tall statue. "Look, it's Pocahontas!"

Sam noticed that the statue was a bronze color, but both Pocahontas's hands were copper colored. That was weird. "Why did they make her hands a different color?" he asked.

Grace smiled. "It's all made of the same bronze, but so many people rub her hands, they've become discolored over time."

"Why do they rub her hands?" asked Caitlin.

"People believe it can give them good luck," replied Grace.

Derek ran over and rubbed one of the statue's hands. "Does it work?"

Sam frowned. "It's just a legend, Derek."

Derek shrugged his shoulders. "Well, it's worth a try. Maybe it will help me uncover something amazing in the dig."

Sam considered his brother's words and quickly gave the statue's palm a quick touch as they passed by. Hey, it couldn't hurt.

They walked into the old church, its entrance marked by a crumbling brick doorway in the remains of a two-story bell tower. A flurry of work was going on inside the church. Parts of the floor were removed and replaced with glass to reveal previous layers of a brick foundation. A man worked in a corner, staring intently at a flat stone slab set on a wooden cart. He operated under a bright light and was working methodically on the edge of the gray slab with a fine tool.

"What's he doing?" Sam asked.

"That's the Knight's Tomb," said Toby. "It might be the oldest colonial gravestone in America."

Sam looked more closely at the massive slab. A shield was engraved in a corner, but in the middle was a large image of an armed figure. "It does look like a knight, I guess."

"Whose grave is it?" asked Caitlin.

"That's what the team has been working to find out," said the man working at the stone, looking up at their group. "Our best guess is a man named Sir

George Yeardley, who was buried in Jamestown in 1627."

Toby nodded. "Historians found a will from one of his relatives that spoke about the broken tomb, so we think it's him."

The man pointed at the gravestone. "This marker had been resting in concrete here in the church floor since 1905. We chiseled it out of the cement by hand, then got it up on this table to work on it."

Sam studied the stone, noticing several places where it had been cracked and pieced back together. "Looks pretty heavy."

The man chuckled. "Heavy is right. Weighs more than twelve-hundred pounds."

"How'd you get it up there on the table?" asked Derek.

"Very carefully," answered the man. "We actually used similar techniques to the ancient Egyptians with rollers and ramps."

"Did you drop it?" asked Sam. "Is that why it's cracked?"

The man laughed. "Thankfully, no. It was already broken in a few spots, but we're preserving it the best we can."

"That's amazing," said Caitlin. Sam thought it was pretty amazing, too.

"Thanks, Jack," Toby said to the man before leading

them out the side door of the church. "The original church was over there in the center of the fort."

Sam saw a fence in the shape of a triangle. It looked rather flimsy to be the wall of a fort. No wonder the Indians attacked them. The distinctive three-sided fort design looked familiar, but he couldn't quite place where he'd seen it. He looked over at Toby and found his answer.

"Is that the fort on your hat?" Sam pointed to a triangle-shaped drawing on Toby's hat.

Toby pulled it off and nodded. "That's right. This is the logo for our Jamestown Rediscovery Project."

"Is that a picture of the fort?" asked Caitlin.

"Yep," answered Toby. "From a map, actually. It was based off a sketch from Captain John Smith."

"What's the 'X' in the middle of the fort?" asked Sam, pointing at the hat. "Is that where they buried the treasure?"

"No," said Toby. "We believe that marks the location of the church."

"But the church is over there," said Caitlin, pointing to the red brick building they'd just left. "And it's outside the fort walls. How could that be?"

"True," said Toby. "But that isn't the original church. The original settlers' church was right over here." He walked to an area in the middle of the fort that had been excavated, the outline of a rectangular building clearly marked.

"I like how he drew a flag," said Derek, pointing to a flag-looking shape sticking out of the edge of the fort drawing on the hat.

"Was that flag for England?" asked Caitlin.

"Once again, looks can be deceiving," said Toby. "What appears to be a flag is actually believed to be a map of a garden or some other building."

Sam's head was starting to spin. All this archaeology mixed with history was complicated. It was cool, but confusing. He walked past the church toward the water. A tall statue labeled as Captain John Smith sat on a gray stone pedestal. Sam looked up at his face, a greenish-color metal like the Statue of Liberty. Sam followed Smith's gaze out across the James River. It was hard to believe that the colonists had sailed to that very spot four hundred years ago. They probably had no idea what they were getting into.

Had the Indians been watching from the bushes, or was that was just something Sam had seen in the movies? Either way, neither group could possibly have imagined their future in this new land. That's what Sam loved about history, learning about what had happened and tracing stories back to where they began.

# CHAPTER FIVE

S am crouched in the hole in the ground. It wasn't a hole really, but an excavation pit. The dig site was divided up into several of them, each a square of roughly ten feet by ten feet. The one he was in sank nearly five feet deep. It reminded him of a large hot tub without any water. Toby said the dig areas were made that way so they could be covered more easily during bad weather. Sam imagined how it might actually fill up like a pool if there was a big storm. Narrow walkways of dirt were left to separate the different digs. The walkways looked like the cinder-block foundation of a house, except with dirt instead of block. But most importantly, the work was tearing things down instead of building them up.

Sam watched Toby working a few feet from him, slowly scraping at the dirt with a trowel that was very much like the kind Mom used for planting flowers in the garden. For some of the finer work, he used small picks and brushes. It was slow going, but Toby said it was important to be careful. You never knew when something might surface, and you didn't want to damage anything.

The soil was brown clay with only a few rocks, but it was hard and packed. Toby had shown him how different colors of soil meant different things. Some soil was original to the wall foundation, while other soil was *fill*, dirt that had been piled on over the centuries. The goal was to move away the fill dirt and carve out the form of the original structure. It was like peeling back the layers of an onion.

Sam lifted his head and surveyed the site. He thought it might take another four hundred years to dig out the whole thing if all they used was a trowel and a toothbrush, but no one seemed too worried about it. The professional archeologists and even the college students like Grace and Toby worked patiently. Patience must be an important quality in this line of work.

Caitlin dug with Grace in the square next to his. The two girls were talking away. Caitlin was asking a million questions about everything, trying to fill up her brain with as much knowledge as possible. It didn't seem like she'd lost any of her enthusiasm.

Sam tried to spot Derek further over in a different section, but he was out of sight. He was probably goofing around. Sam didn't expect his brother to be as interested in the work as he and Caitlin were. Derek liked the idea of being at Field School and of acting like a college kid, but it usually took him a while to get serious.

Sam stopped to wipe the sweat from his forehead. The sun's rays felt good on his bare arms, but he knew the afternoon would grow even warmer. Toby said they'd move shade canopies in if things got too hot. Sam looked around the dig squares, full of nothing but dirt. Despite all the evidence supposedly in the Archaearium, he was starting to wonder if anything really was in this ground after all.

He crouched back down, sinking his trowel into the dirt pointed end first, poking a little deeper than he'd intended. He glanced up quickly to see if Toby had noticed. Even though he was getting tired, he'd didn't want to get yelled at for doing it wrong. Could they kick someone out of Field School for ruining the dig site? He doubted it, but there was a first time for everything.

Toby was busy brushing an angled chunk of earth and didn't seem to notice the mistake, so Sam gave his shovel a quick tug, breaking off a large chunk of clay. He brushed it to the side with his hand, then smoothed off the hole to make it look less obvious. He stopped, turning his head as something caught his attention in the bottom corner of the crevice.

A glint of blue sparkled faintly in the sunlight. Any kind of color stood out amongst all the brown dirt. Sam held his breath, his heart beating faster. He looked back at Toby, but he was still distracted with his brushing. Slowly, Sam reached down to rub the spot with his finger, then thought better of it and used a brush from his pack like Toby was doing. The speck of blue grew slightly larger, sinking deeper and wider into the ground as he brushed.

"Uh, Toby," Sam called.

"Yeah?"

"I think..." He paused, trying to decide what exactly he was going to say. "I think I found something."

Toby set down his brush and scooted toward Sam. "Whacha got?"

"Something's here," said Sam. "Something blue."

Toby pulled off his sunglasses, leaning in closer. "Hmm. Back up for a minute, Sam. Let me take a look at that."

Sam scooted back, allowing Toby to move into his place. Toby leaned close to the ground, pulling a small scalpel-like knife from his belt, and softly worked around the edges of the object. "Well, will ya look at that," he muttered.

Sam watched over Toby's shoulder, his eyes growing larger with each movement Toby made. "What is it?" he asked.

"I don't know." Toby switched back and forth from his scalpel to his brush. "It looks ceramic. The color is similar to some other pieces we've found over near the fort." He sat up and looked at Sam. "But we haven't found anything like that here in the West Wall before." He grinned mischievously. "You might have found something here, Sammy."

Sam's stomach did a somersault. He hoped it was something spectacular, but honestly he would be happy for anything besides more dirt and rocks.

"Hey, Grace," Toby called across to the other dig square. "Come over here a second."

Grace stepped across the center path and down into their square. "What is it?"

Caitlin followed behind like a junior apprentice. She looked at Sam. "Did you find something?"

He nodded, not sure what more to say.

"I think he did," answered Toby. "It looks ceramic to me, possibly Persian. It's the right time period. But take a look and see what you make of it."

Grace moved into the space where Toby had been working and stared at the object. "Man," she muttered, working the edges. The blue pattern continued to grow larger. "It's big."

Sam tilted his head. "Is that good?"

"Well, it depends what it is," said Toby. "But bigger is usually better. Most things in the ground this long are in pieces. It's unusual to pull something out still fully intact."

For the next hour, the team chipped away at the dirt around the object. They let Sam, Caitlin, and even Derek, when he came over midway through, do some of the work. It was painstakingly slow as they made sure no pieces broke or cracked.

Sam watched as two of the other team members measured the location of the object using what they called a Laser Transit and a Stadia Rod. The Transit shot a laser beam across the dig site to the Rod, reflecting off the long vertical pole with red and white length measurements that looked a little like a candy cane. Toby said that the measurement of the beam gave precise directions for 3D mapping of the entire site.

The sun moved lower in the afternoon sky, and the open field turned a golden yellow as the light reflected across the river. Sam got goose bumps. All this reminded him of the scene in the Map Room in *Raiders of the Lost Ark* when Indiana Jones was finding the location of the secret chamber. As Grace freed the object from the last piece of dirt, Sam couldn't help but imagine what was happening when it first found its way into that spot hundreds of years ago.

"It's amazing," said Caitlin, her face filled with awe.

"I can't believe we found it after all this time," said Sam. I can't believe *I* found it, he thought to himself, welling with pride. "What is it? A bowl? A pot?"

"We won't know for sure until it gets cleaned up," Grace said. "My guess is some sort of jug or vase."

"It's a real treasure, whatever it is." Carefully, Toby lifted the pottery from the ground and placed it into a small padded crate.

"We'll take it to the lab to get cleaned up," Grace explained. "You won't believe how much better it will look once all the dirt is removed from the edges."

"Do you think it's valuable?" asked Derek.

Toby smiled. "Derek, all the items we find here at Jamestown are priceless."

Derek frowned. "So they're not worth anything?"

Grace laughed. "No, it means they're irreplaceable."

"It's a part of how our country began," said Toby. "You can't put a price tag on that."

Sam smiled, getting goose bumps again.

Caitlin nudged his arm, noticing his grin. "Proud of yourself?"

"Yep," said Sam. "It's pretty sweet."

# CHAPTER SIX

Later that afternoon, Toby brought Sam to see Marcus Emerson, the chief laboratory scientist at Historic Jamestown. Toby said Marcus had worked on archaeological digs and expeditions all over the world, in Mexico, Peru, and even Egypt! Unlike the rest of the team, he spent most of his time back in the lab. That seemed a lot more boring to Sam, but he didn't say so.

"This is where we do the real discovery, Sam," explained Marcus, a wiry man with thinning black hair and glasses. He was a lot more like what Sam had pictured a scientist to look like than most of the team at Jamestown.

"How's that?"

"Well, while the rest of the team is out digging through the dirt, I get to the heart of matters." Marcus turned to several metal shelves against the wall filled with assorted containers, bins and baskets. "Everything the team digs up comes here to the lab where we clean, analyze, categorize, and date each item. There are thousands of them."

"Sounds like a lot of work," said Sam, looking over the lab. In addition to the shelves, there were cabinets and tables, all made of stainless steel like in a restaurant kitchen. One workstation had a microscope and other delicate-looking instruments; another seemed more like a craftsman's table with paintbrushes and other small tools. He looked up at the ceiling and noticed large silver vents. "Is that the air-conditioning?"

"In a sense," said Marcus. "This room is controlled to keep the humidity levels constant. It helps the artifacts stay in pristine condition. The doors are monitored, with alarms that go off if they are open too long."

Sam spied another piece of equipment with a metal frame and an expensive-looking camera mounted to the top. "Is that for taking pictures of the artifacts?"

Marcus nodded. "Exactly. It's part of the cataloguing system. Everything that comes out of the ground is photographed so we have complete records. We're very methodical about things here. Everything has its place."

Probably a good idea, thought Sam. He'd never remember all the different items that had been discovered. He often forgot where he'd put things in his bedroom back home, and they hadn't even been buried in the ground. He wondered if anything ever got mixed up here, despite all their systems.

In the middle of the room was a large table with a sink and more power tools. "What's all this?"

"We have just the right tool for each particular item," replied Marcus. "Some are small, some are large. This table is used for water screening, which sifts the artifacts from the hundreds of years of mud and grime. We can get down to the base level and see what's really there. Find the diamond in the rough, if you will."

Sam's eyes lit up. "Diamonds?"

Marcus chuckled. "Not literally, of course. Often we only find small items like turtle shells, or brass tacks and rivets, but sometimes we have larger items that require more delicate methods. Here, let me show you an example." He stepped over to the table and picked up something the size of a basketball. He held it out to Sam. "What would you say this is?"

It didn't look like much at all to Sam except a dark brown clump of dirt. "A rock?"

Marcus chuckled. "You might think so." He set it back down on the table. "But after centuries of dirt and corrosion are stripped away, sometimes we can uncover something incredible." He walked over to the nearest shelf, reaching into a basket. "Like this." He held a shiny bronze helmet like the kind a soldier would wear.

Sam's eyebrows rose. It didn't look anything like the

clump of mud. "There's a helmet inside that dirty clump?"

Marcus smiled. "Could be. I uncovered this helmet from a grouping of earth just like the one on the table several weeks ago. So you see what I mean about us making discoveries here in the lab as well?"

Sam nodded. It did seem pretty cool, although he still thought he'd rather be out in the field hunting for treasure on the front lines. "Where's the piece that I found today?"

"Ah, yes." Marcus nodded, stepping over to the counter on the wall. "I nearly forgot. Quite a find for your first day of digging."

Sam smiled, remembering the excitement he'd felt when he saw the blue color poking out from the dirt. Marcus pointed to the counter where he had the item in a small padded box with a light over it.

"Do you know what it is?" asked Sam.

Marcus flicked the light on. "Certainly a type of pottery. I'd say a vase made from a sixteenth-century ceramic. Most likely Persian, Toby may have been right about that part, but from the northern regions if I had to guess. We'll need to study it some more to be sure. Quite valuable, no doubt, even in its own day."

He took a small scalpel and used it as a pointer. "See those deep blue specks in the pattern along the side? Each of those are quite intricate—they're the mark of a master craftsman during that time period. It's quite rare, actually. It was probably an item used for special occasions."

"Like my mom's china," said Sam, smiling. He liked how the wavy blue pattern sparkled in the light box. The lines reminded him of a small fish swimming upstream against the brown background of the pottery. It was beautiful.

"Can I take a picture of it?" Sam pulled his phone from his pocket. He was anxious to use his new device as much as possible.

"No!" barked Marcus, suddenly. "No photographs." He shook his head. "I'm sorry, but we have very strict rules about what gets photographed before it's on display. Rest assured, we'll have it properly documented, but we can't allow any outside photos."

Sam's eyes opened wide, surprised by Marcus' quick rebuke. "That's okay. I don't want to get you in trouble." He was hoping to send a picture home to his parents to show what he'd found on the dig site. He looked back at his vase and tried to hide his disappointment. "What will you do with it now?"

"First, we'll sit it in a delicate chemical bath to wash away most of the remaining contaminants," answered Marcus, seeming to calm down.

"And then will it be put in a museum?"

"Once we document and catalog it, then we'll likely display it over in the Archaearium, or perhaps it might be of interest to another museum like the Smith—" Marcus stopped himself, glancing hesitantly at Sam. "It will probably be in the Archaearium," he repeated, after a pause.

No matter where it was displayed, Sam thought it was pretty cool that something he'd discovered would be in the museum for people to see. He looked over at Marcus and wondered if he was acting a bit strangely.

An electronic beep sounded as the door opened. Toby's voice came from the doorway. "Marcus, there's a truck outside delivering some equipment that needs your signature." He looked across the room. "How's it going in here, Sam? Getting the inside scoop?"

Sam waved. "Yep."

"Fantastic. That must be my new imaging console." Marcus glanced at Sam hesitantly. "I'll be right back. Don't touch anything."

"No problem," said Sam. After the door beeped behind Marcus, Sam looked back at his vase. He wished he could tell somebody else about it. He didn't know why they needed a no-picture-taking policy. It was probably for other kinds of people, since it wasn't like he was going to sell pictures of the artifacts to the tabloids or anything. He glanced back over his shoulder at the closed door, then without thinking about it any further, he pulled out his phone and took several pictures of the vase.

The lab door beeped open and Marcus' voice came from behind him. "That sounds good, Toby. Thank you."

Sam jumped at the sound, setting his phone down on the counter by the wall and stepping away, trying to look casual. He felt hot around his shirt collar and felt his face turn red. He didn't want to get in trouble. That was Derek's specialty, not his.

"Sam, clear that table for me, will you?" Marcus asked, carrying a large cardboard box. Sam scrambled over and moved a stack of papers.

"Well I guess I should go meet the others," Sam said quickly, turning toward the door and hoping he wasn't sweating. "Thanks for showing me around, Marcus. It's really cool."

Marcus nodded, setting the box down on the counter. "You're welcome, Sam. Great work today."

Sam hustled out the door, leaving the lab behind. He wove through the building to get to the parking lot where Derek and Caitlin were waiting.

# CHAPTER SEVEN

S am felt exhausted by the time they finally boarded
the shuttle bus to the college to get cleaned up for a
late dinner. Spending hours in the dirt under the sun was
tiring enough, but with all the extra excitement of finding
his artifact, he was ready to crash.

After showering and changing back in their dorms,
the boys met up with Caitlin and walked to the college
cafeteria. Sam set his tray of food down at one of the
round tables and slid into a chair next to Caitlin.

"Hungry?" she asked, looking at his overflowing
plate.

"Starving."

"Ouch, Sam," said Derek, sitting on the other side.
"Don't say that after being at Jamestown all day."

Caitlin grimaced. "I'm trying not to think about the
whole Starving Time and eating people part."

"Do you think that's really true?" asked Sam.

Caitlin shrugged. "I guess. It seems to be supported by scientific evidence. Professor Evanshade wouldn't make something like that up."

"This food's not bad, huh?" said Derek.

Sam's eyes were bulging at the huge assortment of choices on his tray. "Not bad? This is like Thanksgiving!" He'd had a tough time deciding what not to take from the several different food stations. There were hot foods and sandwiches, pastas, burgers, salads, and a whole section of desserts including pie and five flavors of ice cream.

Caitlin giggled. "I think we might have a hard time getting Sam to leave."

"Hey, I told you I was hungry," Sam replied as he dug into a big helping of mashed potatoes.

"It's kind of unfair," said Caitlin.

"What do you mean?" asked Derek.

"You know, all this food." She waved her arm across the cafeteria. "The settlers in Jamestown barely had anything. I think we just take all this for granted."

Derek nodded. "Yeah, I guess you're right. I've never really thought about that before."

"We're lucky," mumbled Sam between bites of delicious mac and cheese.

"Very," agreed Caitlin.

"Speaking of lucky," said Derek, "I can't believe you found that pottery in the dig today."

Sam smiled, happy that he'd been the one to find it and not his brother. Most of the time it seemed like Derek did everything first. It was nice to turn the tables for a change. "It was skill, not luck," Sam replied, imitating something his brother would say. "Toby said I'm a natural archeologist."

Derek frowned. "Whatever. Let's not get carried away."

Caitlin laughed. "What did you see in the lab? Did they let you clean the artifact that you found?"

Sam finished chewing and leaned back in his chair. "Not clean it, but I saw all the tools and devices they use." He told them how Marcus showed him around and described the different cataloguing systems and tools.

"Lucky," Derek said again.

"He said they might even display it in a museum," said Sam proudly.

"Like the Archaearium?" asked Caitlin.

"Yeah, or maybe even the Smithsonian," said Sam. "Although Marcus was acting a little peculiar about that. I'm not sure why."

"The Smithsonian? Really?" asked Caitlin.

"Yeah. I'll show you the—" Sam leaned forward and glanced around the table, then quieted to a whisper. "The picture I took of my piece in the lab. I wasn't supposed to, but I snuck it when Marcus left the room."

"Hold on a minute," said Derek. "You did something you weren't supposed to do?"

"It's not a big deal." Sam frowned and reached for his phone in his pocket, but it wasn't there.

"Well?" said Derek.

Sam patted his other pockets, but there was no phone. "That's weird, I had it this afternoon."

Derek shook his head. "Mom is going to kill you if you've lost your new phone already."

"I didn't lose it," replied Sam. He tried to think. "I had it in the lab."

"Did you drop it somewhere?" asked Caitlin.

"Oh, no," Sam moaned.

"What?" said Caitlin.

"I set it down on the counter when Marcus came back in and surprised me." Sam put his hand on his forehead. "I must have left it there."

Derek smirked. "Smooth one, Sam."

"Marcus probably picked it up," said Caitlin reassuringly. "I'm sure he saved it for you. You can just get it tomorrow."

"Yeah, I guess you're right," sighed Sam. He felt foolish for misplacing his new phone so soon.

"Or," said Derek, "we could go back tonight and get

it. You were going to show us the lab anyway. It's perfect."

Sam frowned. "Not exactly perfect. How would we even get over there?"

"It's a little too far to walk," said Caitlin.

Derek grinned, standing up from the table. "Leave that to me." He strode over to the other side of the cafeteria where a group of students from the Field School were eating. He sat for a minute and talked to them, then gestured back to Sam and Caitlin at their table. He high-fived one of the guys and came back over.

"We're all set," said Derek.

Sam raised his eyebrows. "With what?"

"What did you say to them?" asked Caitlin.

"I asked if anyone was free to give us a ride back over to Jamestown this evening, and Patrick said he was going that direction and it was no problem."

"He did?" asked Sam. He remembered that Patrick worked in the Archaearium, but hadn't really met him yet.

Derek nodded. "Yeah. I told you I'd take care of it. It's a gift."

Sam didn't say so, but he was often impressed with how Derek could talk people into things. Usually he was talking Sam into doing something to get him in trouble, but sometimes Derek's mouth actually came in handy.

"And I think Grace likes me," Derek added.

Sam made a face at Caitlin and started laughing. "You think what?"

"I think she likes me," Derek repeated, a cocky grin on his face. "I told you the college girls dig the younger man type."

"Sure they do," mocked Sam. "You're only, what, seven years younger than she is?"

"Ten," said Caitlin. "I think she's in graduate school."

"Okay, laugh at me if you want to," said Derek.

"Oh, don't worry, I will," said Sam.

"Well, either way, I want to see the lab too," said Caitlin. "I guess it would be okay to do it tonight, since you do need to get your phone."

"Great," said Derek. "Then let's go!"

# CHAPTER EIGHT

"Thanks for the ride," said Sam, as Patrick drove along the dark road that led between Williamsburg and Jamestown. If it hadn't been for the car they were riding in, Sam might have thought he was back in colonial times. As they pulled out of Williamsburg, the sign said the road was called the *Colonial Parkway*. It didn't have any painted lines and was paved with some kind of brown, stony mixture.

"Not a problem," Patrick replied. "I need to log a few things into the computer in my office over at the Archaearium anyway."

"We shouldn't be long," said Derek. "Sam just forgot his phone in the lab."

Sam shot Derek a look. He didn't need to have Patrick and everyone else knowing that he was irresponsible.

"Have you guys been to the Archaearium yet?" asked Patrick, seeming to ignore Derek's comment.

"No," said Caitlin, "but I'd like to."

Patrick nodded. "You should walk over after you get Sam's phone and have a look. It's worth it. I'll leave the back door unlocked while I'm there."

Caitlin glanced over at Sam, who nodded. It did sound kind of interesting. "Do you run the whole place and get to choose which items end up on display?"

"No," chuckled Patrick. "But I am working under Doc's supervision as part of my graduate program internship. I work a lot with Doc and Marcus to determine which artifacts are most appropriate for the Archaearium and which might get sent out to other places. It's only temporary, at least for now. I'm hoping to stay on full-time after grad school, or if not here, then maybe at another museum. "

"Wow," said Caitlin. "That would be a cool job."

Sam raised his eyebrows at her comment. Working all day in a museum seemed a little slow to him, but Caitlin would probably like it.

"Do you send pieces to the Smithsonian?" asked Sam.

"Sometimes, but I've only sent a couple so far," replied Patrick.

As they drove onto the island, Sam noticed a light in a small building off the road among the trees. It was the Glasshouse; he remembered that from when they first arrived. It seemed odd that people would be working so late, but they must work long hours. Maybe glass came out better at night? He made a mental note to check it out before the week was over.

They pulled into the parking lot and followed Patrick to the back of the lab building. He unlocked the door. "I'll be at the Archaearium. Just walk over when you're done here. This door locks by itself, so just pull it closed when you leave." He paused, then looked at them seriously. "And don't touch anything, okay? Marcus would have a heart attack."

They nodded and filed into the hallway as Patrick vanished into the darkness. Sam opened the door to the lab, the familiar air-lock sound greeting them, and then flipped on the light switch. Bright overhead lights lit up the room, while a few smaller table LEDs cast a glow over the workstations.

"Whoa, this is cool," said Derek, stepping over to the table with the washing device. "It's like a mad scientist's laboratory."

"Hands off," warned Sam. "I don't want to get in trouble."

Derek made a "who me" face, like he was insulted. Sam walked over to the equipment station where he'd left his phone. He leaned over the counter but it was empty. He closed his eyes. Mom was going to kill him, just like Derek had said.

"Take me to your leader!"

Sam turned around to see Derek wearing a black gas mask that covered his whole face. He walked toward them with his arms stretched out like something out of a science fiction movie.

"Take that off!" shouted Sam.

Derek laughed as he pulled the mask over his head. "Geez, Sam. Chill out. You didn't seem so concerned about the rules when you were taking pictures earlier."

"I told you, don't say anything about that," said Sam. If Derek didn't keep his big mouth shut, someone was going to hear. It figured that the one time Sam broke the rules, it would come back to haunt him.

Caitlin shook her head. "All right, guys. Sam, do you see your phone?"

Sam shook his head.

"Is this it?" asked Derek, holding a phone in his hand.

Sam's eyes brightened. "Yes! Where did you find it?"

"It was over here by the computer."

"Marcus must have found it," said Caitlin.

Sam let out a deep breath. "Thanks," he said, taking the phone.

"No problem. It's—"

"A gift, yeah, yeah, I know," said Sam, cutting him off. He was glad Derek had found it, but didn't need his brother going on again about how great he was.

"So what is all this stuff?" asked Caitlin.

Sam pointed out the different equipment and stations that Marcus had shown him. He looked for his discovery, but it wasn't where Marcus had placed it before. It must have been moved to another room.

"Pretty cool," said Derek.

A high-pitched alarm rang out in the room, followed by a computerized voice. "Attention. Humidity levels rising. Please check door lock."

Sam's eyes opened wide as he turned to Derek. "Oh my gosh. Did you shut the door?"

Derek gave his best dummy look. "I don't know. I think Caitlin was the last one in."

Rolling her eyes, Caitlin walked over and pulled the door shut. "That should fix it."

Sam heard the door seal as the alarm turned off. "Marcus is going to kill us if we mess up the humidity levels."

"Luckily, he's going to be killing you already for taking the picture," said Derek.

Sam looked at the door and then remembered Patrick. "We should probably head over to the Archaearium."

"Right," said Caitlin. "I'm excited to see it."

Sam flipped the switch for the lights and closed the door securely behind them.

Outside, Sam strained his eyes to adjust to the darkness. A few security lights shone along the path, but everything looked very different than it had in the daytime.

"The Archaearium's this way, right?" asked Caitlin, pointing toward the water.

Sam nodded. He remembered having seen it when they'd headed to the West Wall.

"Just follow the path," said Derek, already walking ahead. They glimpsed the outline of the brick church ahead to the left, then turned to the right toward the Archaearium building. Another floodlight illuminated a back door. Sam wasn't sure where Patrick's office was, but the door was unlocked, and they quietly entered.

"Which way?" asked Derek.

"I want to see the artifacts," said Caitlin.

They walked until they came to a dimly lit room filled with cases and displays.

"Wow," said Sam.

"Do you really think all of this came out of the ground right here where we're digging?" asked Derek.

Caitlin nodded. "It's all from Jamestown. Not just by the West Wall, but by the fort, the church, all around."

"Don't wander too far," said Sam. "We don't want to get lost in here." He stared into the nearest display case, which was filled with old coins, rusted spears, tools, and helmets. He thought back to his experience seeing the pottery gleaming from the dirt and imagined what it must have been like to find so many of these different items. One of the glass cases had shelves of pottery that looked similar to the piece he'd found, although none of it had the same cool, wavy patterns.

"Guys, look at this," called Derek from around the corner. Sam and Caitlin joined him next to a flat display case in the middle of the floor. The room was mostly dark, but something was laid out inside the case.

"Oh my gosh," said Sam, realizing he was looking at a skeleton. He read the sign on the wall. "*Jane*. One of the recovered remains that shows evidence of cannibalism amongst the colonists."

"That is so sad," said Caitlin. "Can you imagine being so desperate for food that you had to resort to eating someone else?"

Sam made a face like he had a bad taste in his mouth. It was sad, but it was also disgusting. He really didn't want to think about it.

"I always pictured cannibals like headhunters or something on a tropical island, not at a colonial fort," said Derek. "Caitlin, if you were starving and had no other option, who would you eat first, me or Sam?"

Sam closed his eyes wearily. Leave it to his brother to ask a question like that.

"Neither," answered Caitlin, laughing nervously. "I'd eat a belt."

"A belt?" asked Derek. "That wasn't one of the options."

She pointed to another display sign. "It says that during the Starving Time, some people boiled their leather belts for food."

Sam shook his head. "That doesn't sound very good either."

"Better than eating a person," said Caitlin.

A loud bang from somewhere in the building echoed through the room.

Sam looked around the display case. "What was that?"

"It sounded like a door slamming," said Caitlin.

"Patrick?" called Sam, softly.

"He said he'd be in his office," said Caitlin.

"Where's his office?" asked Derek.

Caitlin shrugged. "Beats me."

"Yo, Patrick!" called Derek obnoxiously.

"Shh," scolded Sam, looking around. He didn't think there were security guards or anything, but he didn't want to get in trouble for being there.

"What? There's nobody here." Derek glanced back over his shoulder, then moved close to Sam's ear. "Except for...*Jane.*"

Sam's eyes bulged as he pushed Derek away.

"But I don't think she'll mind," Derek continued.

Sam looked back at the old skeleton in the case beside

them. A shiver ran down his spine. All these things were cool, but he was starting to wish that they'd come in the daytime. "We should get out of here," he said.

"He's right," said Caitlin. "Patrick's not here, and we need to find him so we still have a ride home." She walked toward the doorway. "Let's go."

# CHAPTER NINE

S am didn't think they'd been inside the Archaearium very long, but when they stepped back outside, the night seemed darker. A strong breeze was blowing in across the dig site from the river. He glanced around at the deserted area and the hairs stood up on the back of his neck. "This feels weird."

"It does, somehow, doesn't it?" Caitlin looked up and down the path. "Where is Patrick?"

"I don't know," said Sam.

"Maybe he went back to the lab to look for us," said Derek. "Let's head back there."

They nodded and headed back the way they'd come. It seemed like all the floodlights on the path had been turned off, so they went slowly in the darkness.

Sam stopped at the sound of a branch breaking in the

distance. He peered through the darkness, but didn't see anything.

"What's wrong?" asked Caitlin.

"I thought I heard something," said Sam.

"Maybe it was Patrick," said Derek. He raised his hands to his mouth, about to call out, when Sam stopped him.

"Hold on," Sam whispered. "Look over there." He pointed toward the old brick church.

"What is it?" asked Caitlin quietly.

"And why are we whispering?" said Derek.

Sam crouched lower. "I think I saw a shadow moving along the trail. Someone's over there."

"I told you, it's probably Patrick." Derek moved next to him with Caitlin.

"I don't think so," said Sam. "Patrick is taller."

"Well then, it's someone else," said Derek. "What's the big deal?" He began to stand again when Sam grabbed hold of his arm.

"Wait," said Sam, still whispering. A light, like a small flame, flickered directly under the entrance to the crumbling tower at the front of the brick church.

"There's two of them," whispered Caitlin.

"Something's going on," Sam said.

"There's only one way to find out what," said Derek impatiently. He moved forward, still in a crouch, slinking stealthily toward the light.

"Hold on," Sam whispered fiercely. But it was too late. As usual, Derek was jumping into things without thinking them through. Sam liked to consider all the options first, but most of the time with Derek around he didn't get the chance.

"Come on," said Caitlin, inching forward. "It might be vandals. We can't let them destroy any of the dig. It's too important."

Sam hadn't thought of that. As Caitlin moved out of sight, he tried to block out his fears and followed behind. He didn't like the idea of her being braver than he was.

It was hard to see through the darkness without a flashlight, but Sam managed to navigate the pathway toward the old church. He finally glimpsed Derek and Caitlin crouching together behind the Pocahontas statue.

"Do you see anything?" Sam asked.

"Shh," said Derek, waving with his hand to stay down. "They're in the church. Something's going down."

Sam listened. Through the darkness he could faintly hear voices inside the church, but he couldn't make out what they were saying. Every few moments, a red-orange glow showed through the window, like one of the people was smoking. "I can't hear anything."

"Or see anything," said Caitlin.

"We have to get closer," whispered Derek. He crept ahead, low to the ground, until he was against the outside of the church tower. He stood slowly, staying close to the wall, then slipped inside. Sam tried to remember what the church tower looked like in the light. It was two stories high, square, roughly six feet across, and it served as the entranceway to the main church. He imagined that Derek would be able to hide in the darkness without being spotted. Whether he'd be able to see or hear anything was another matter.

"This is crazy," Sam whispered to Caitlin. He looked up at the Pocahontas statue, the moonlight reflecting off her copper-colored hands. It was the second time he'd visited the statue, and he wondered if it was bringing him any luck.

"I can't see him," said Caitlin. Before either could speak further, they saw movement. The orange light moved out the side door of the church, walking briskly away from where they hid and toward the riverbank further up the island. He seemed to be carrying something, but it was too dark to tell what it was.

Sam held his breath, waiting for the other shadow to emerge. Derek had better keep himself hidden. After nearly a minute, he was about to tell Caitlin that something must have happened when a shadow stepped out of the front entrance of the tower. It was too tall to be Derek, and it was still too dark to see a face. Derek must have managed to stay unnoticed, because the figure continued up the path toward the lab.

"Where's Derek?" Caitlin whispered.

"There's no telling," muttered Sam. The coast seemed to be clear, but he didn't want to risk moving yet in case anyone else was lurking. Maybe there were other people they hadn't seen besides the two in the church. Derek must have been thinking similarly, because just when Sam was starting to think it might be safe, he emerged as another shadow from the church tower and hurried over to them.

"Are you okay?" asked Sam.

Derek nodded, his face serious.

"What's the matter?" asked Caitlin. "Did you hear them?"

Derek nodded again. "Some of it, but only one of them spoke. It was too dark to see their faces, and the person who came out the front door didn't say anything. That one just handed a box to the other one, who handed something back." He let out a long breath. "One walked right past me in the tower."

"You shouldn't have gotten that close," said Sam. "It was stupid."

"We need to get out of here," said Caitlin. "Patrick is probably looking for us."

"Maybe that *was* Patrick," said Sam, feeling unnerved by the whole situation. He wondered how their fun week of camp could have turned so creepy so quickly.

They stood and began walking back toward the lab.

As they rounded the obelisk, a dark figure suddenly appeared on the path in front of them. "There you guys are!"

Sam nearly jumped out of his skin. It was Grace.

"You nearly scared me to death," exclaimed Caitlin.

"What are you doing out here?" Grace asked.

"We were—" began Sam, until Derek poked him discretely in the side.

"We were coming back from the Archaearium," Derek said. "Patrick was supposed to be down there, but we never found him."

"What are *you* doing here?" asked Caitlin.

Grace nodded, like something made sense. "I was doing rounds up in the dorms and couldn't find you. Someone said they'd heard Patrick tell Derek at dinner that he'd take you over here. I tried to call your phone, Sam, but it went straight to voice mail, and I don't have Derek's number."

"The battery must be dead," said Sam, feeling the weight of the phone in his pocket.

"We're ready to go," said Derek, stepping toward the lab.

"Great," said Grace. "Then let's get you all back to the dorm. I'm not sure what Doc's policy on your being over here at night is, but it's probably not the greatest idea to be wandering around in the dark."

Sam wanted to ask Grace about what they'd seen at the church, but he knew from Derek's look that he wanted to keep it quiet. Derek usually wanted to try to figure things out on their own.

# CHAPTER TEN

The ride back in the car with Grace was mostly quiet. Sam was tired from the busy day, and they all seemed unsure of what they'd actually seen at the church. Back at the college, they said good night to Grace and huddled on the brick steps outside Caitlin's dorm.

"So?" asked Sam, after sitting for a few seconds without anyone saying anything. A dim porch light shone just enough so he could see everyone's faces.

"So what?" replied Derek.

"So, what in the world was that all about?" continued Sam. "Who was that in the church?"

"And what were they talking about?" added Caitlin.

Derek shook his head. "I couldn't see. It was too dark. But like I said, it was some kind of exchange. The only thing I heard one of them say was, 'See you again soon.'"

"Which person said that?" asked Sam. "The one who walked past you in the tower, or the one who was smoking and went out the back door?"

"The back door," said Derek. "I couldn't see him at all, only hear him."

"Didn't the other one walk right past you?" Sam didn't know how his brother could have missed seeing them. What was the point of risking going in there if he wasn't even going to look?

"It was pitch black in that entranceway," said Derek.

"Why would two people be sneaking around in the shadows like that?" asked Caitlin.

"So they could trade whatever that was in secret," said Derek.

"I think we should tell Professor Evanshade," said Sam. "It might have something to do with why he was acting weird the other day on the phone."

"That's right," said Caitlin. "We still don't know what that was all about." She looked at Sam. "You think they're connected?"

"Beats me," said Sam. "But maybe."

"They could be," said Derek, "but we can't tell the professor. Not yet."

Sam frowned. His brother never wanted to tell anybody about anything. It usually got them into trouble of some sort. "Why shouldn't we tell him?" he asked, even though he knew what Derek would say.

"Because I want to figure all this out before we tell him."

"It might be dangerous," said Sam.

Derek waved his hand. "More dangerous than the poachers at Maymont?"

"Well..." started Sam.

"Or the alligators at The Jefferson? Or the hidden treasure in the coal mine?"

"That was different," said Sam.

"Admit it, Sam," Derek said with a huff, "the only reason anything exciting ever happens is because we keep trying to discover things. Waiting around isn't going to do it. Don't you want to have adventures?"

"Of course I do, but you know what I mean."

"I don't think I do," continued Derek, narrowing his eyes, "because we end up having this conversation every time something exciting is about to happen."

"Okay you guys," interrupted Caitlin. "Let's slow down and review what's really going on here. We need to know why Professor Evanshade was upset before we can determine if what we saw in the church is connected. We don't even know those people were doing anything wrong. Maybe they were just two people talking."

"In the dark, at a historic church in Jamestown?" asked Derek. "Sure, that sounds like a great place to chat to me."

Sam tried to think of other ways to explain what they

had witnessed. "We'll see. But if we see any more freaky things like tonight, then we're telling someone."

Caitlin nodded. "Agreed."

"Makes sense," said Derek.

Sam frowned. Just because something *made* sense to Derek didn't mean the three of them would end up doing the sensible thing.

# CHAPTER ELEVEN

S am woke early the next morning just as the sunlight was beginning to stream through the windows. He'd been dreaming about the encounter on the island. Falling asleep, he couldn't stop thinking about the two shadows that had been meeting in the church.

He was also anxious for the day's activities. One of his favorite parts of summer had always been exploring and discovering new things. He couldn't help but wonder what new artifacts would be uncovered at Field Camp. Usually his summers didn't involve digging for ancient relics, but any day he was out exploring and not in school was a good day.

The professor had told them he was going to spend the morning giving them a personal tour around parts of the island they hadn't seen yet, which sounded fun. Behind the scenes access made him feel important.

A buzz sounded from his phone on the dresser. He picked it up to see a text from Toby.

*Doc wants you to stop by his office this AM first thing.*

Sam looked up at Derek, still sleeping in the top bunk. What could the professor want? Maybe he'd heard about their after-hours trip to the lab and the Archaearium. Or maybe he'd found out Sam had taken a picture of the vase. He'd never seemed like the kind of grown-up who would yell at kids, but then again, he did sound upset on the phone when they'd arrived. Whatever it was, Sam hoped their special tour was still on.

As he sat thinking, his phone buzzed once more. This time it was a text from Caitlin.

*Did you get a message from Toby?*

*Yeah*, he typed back.

*What's up?*

*Don't know*

*OK. CU at breakfast?*

*Gotta wake Derek first.*

*LOL. CU Then.*

*Bye*

Sam was still trying to get used to having a phone and texting all the time. He shoved Derek's shoulder and told him to wake up as he walked to the bathroom. He figured it was good that Caitlin had gotten the same message. At least he wasn't getting singled out.

After breakfast, they caught a ride to Jamestown with some other Field School students. The door to the professor's office was closed, but Caitlin pulled off a note stuck to it with a piece of tape.

"It's for us," she said.

"What's it say?" asked Sam.

Caitlin read the note aloud.

*Good morning, kids. I'm sorry, but I was called away unexpectedly today and won't be able to do our tour. I'll make it up to you, I promise. In my absence, however, please head over to the Jamestown Settlement museum. My friend Jada, one of the staff guides, has a special project that I think you'll be perfect for. Thanks, and I'll see you tomorrow. Professor Evanshade.*

"Aw, man," sighed Caitlin. "I was really looking forward to that."

"I know," said Derek. "I couldn't *wait* for some more learning."

Caitlin shot him a nasty glance. "Hey."

"What's he mean by a special assignment?" asked Sam.

"Maybe they have more artifacts for us to uncover," Caitlin said with a glint in her eye.

"Or maybe the janitor is out sick and they need Sam to clean the bathrooms," said Derek, laughing.

"Cut it out," Sam grumbled.

"I don't think he'd ask us to do something that wasn't fun," said Caitlin. "Or at least educational."

"Yeah, but it depends on who's definition of fun we're talking about," said Derek. "And I'm sure Sam could find the toilets very educational."

"Shut up," Sam said again.

"Or maybe he wants me to spend the day with Grace," Derek said.

Sam shook his head. "I don't think she deserves that kind of punishment."

"There's only one way to find out," said Caitlin, turning down the hall.

As Sam followed her, Derek lingered by the office, tapping lightly on the door as he peeked through the small rectangular window above the handle.

"He's not in there," Sam said over his shoulder.

"That's what I'm counting on," said Derek as he turned the handle and the door creaked open.

Sam's eyes widened. There was no limit to Derek's troublemaking. "What are you doing? We shouldn't go in there."

"Toby told us to," replied Derek.

"Not exactly," said Caitlin, walking back to them.

"He texted us that Doc wanted to see us," said Derek, slipping through the doorway. "Well, here we are. We wanted to find clues about his argument on the phone. Remember? Now's our chance."

Sam felt his stomach turn as Derek began nosing around the shelves.

Caitlin sighed. "I should probably make sure he doesn't break anything."

"Wait," started Sam, as she walked inside. "This is stupid," he muttered, glancing both ways in the hall nervously. He hated the feeling he got when he was doing something he wasn't supposed to do. He always felt like he was about to get caught. He didn't even like to watch scenes in movies when someone was about to be found out. His mom told him it was a good thing, that it was his conscience, but Derek called it Sam's chicken self.

"Come on, guys," Sam whispered. "Get out of there."

When no one answered, he poked his head back through the doorway. They were huddled around the professor's desk, staring at something. "Guys?"

Derek waved him over. "Check this out, Sam."

Reluctantly, Sam stepped into the office and glanced around at the cluttered shelves. He wondered how long it had taken the professor to collect everything there. He joined them at the desk. "What's so important?"

"We found a letter," said Derek.

Sam stretched his neck to see over his brother's shoulder and saw an official-looking document on the desk. Fancy letterhead at the top said *The Smithsonian*. He remembered Marcus mentioning the Smithsonian in the lab right before he'd changed the subject. "What does it say?"

Derek looked up to answer when they heard a noise out in the hall. "Go see if anybody's coming," he whispered.

"You just called me in here," Sam protested, but he moved quickly to the door. He certainly didn't want to be found snooping around the professor's office. He turned into the hallway and nearly bumped right into Grace.

"Whoa," Grace exclaimed. "Excuse me there, Sam."

Sam's heart was racing, but he tried to look normal. "Oh, sorry, Grace," he answered loudly so Derek and Caitlin would hear him.

"Did you find Doc?" Grace asked, looking over Sam's shoulder.

"He's not here," Sam mumbled, searching for an explanation just as Derek and Caitlin appeared in the doorway behind him.

"Hey, Grace," said Derek, smiling widely. "Doc left us a note." He nodded at the note in Caitlin's hand.

"We have a special assignment," she added, holding up the piece of paper that had been posted to the door.

"Special assignment?" said Grace, grinning. "Sounds exciting."

"Do you know where we could find an extra toilet plunger?" Derek asked, smirking at Sam.

Sam shot him an evil glare as Grace looked confused.

"Never mind them," sighed Caitlin. "We're supposed to go over to the Jamestown Settlement museum. Can we walk there?"

"It's a bit far to walk," said Grace. "But why don't you use some of the bikes?"

"Bikes?" asked Caitlin.

"You mean like motorcycles?" said Derek, his head perking up. "Cool. I'm a very experienced Harley rider."

Sam groaned. Ever since they'd ridden a couple times on the back of some motorcycles with Mad Dog DeWitt and his gang on another adventure, Derek always acted like he was some kind of motocross champion.

Grace laughed. "Is that right? Well, I'm afraid we only have bicycles, but I think they should still work for you. I think Patrick has them stored over by the Archaearium. Why don't you check with him?"

"That should work fine," said Caitlin. "Come on guys, let's go!" She pushed by Derek playfully as they walked outside.

"Before we get the bikes," said Sam, "I want to ask Patrick if he has my vase ready for display."

"It's not *your* vase, Sam," said Derek.

"I found it."

"Yeah, but it belongs to Jamestown."

Sam frowned. "Well, technically. But it's still special to me." He'd been the one to discover it, whether it was actually his or not. Maybe they'd put a mention of his name on a note card in the display at the Smithsonian, although that was probably asking too much.

# CHAPTER TWELVE

They walked across the lawn to the Archaearium, this time entering through the main doors. A woman at the front table recognized them from Field School and waved them through to the displays. She told them Patrick was by the *Jane* exhibit.

Sam didn't really want to know any more about cannibalism or see the skeleton, so he was relieved when they saw Patrick working on one of the display cases in the main hallway.

"Hi, Patrick," said Derek.

"Oh, hey, guys," Patrick answered.

"Thanks for ditching us last night," said Derek.

Caitlin opened her mouth in surprise. "Derek!"

"I was looking for you all, but..." started Patrick.

"I'm just messing with you, Patrick," laughed Derek. "It's okay. Grace gave us a ride home."

Patrick smiled, seeming to go along with the joke. "That's what I thought. She told me she was going to pick you up."

"Grace told us there are some bikes over here we can ride to the Settlement museum. Do you know where they are?" asked Caitlin.

Patrick stood up. "Sure, I think they're in the green shed behind the building. You're welcome to use them, although I'm not sure when they were ridden last. They might be a little dusty, but I think there's enough for the three of you."

"Cool, thanks," said Derek.

"Did you get a chance to look around the displays at all last night?" Patrick asked, motioning to the artifacts all around them.

Sam's face perked up a little. "Do you have my vase displayed here yet? The one Marcus had in the lab yesterday?"

"I told you, it's not yours, Sam," repeated Derek.

Patrick grinned. "Why, as a matter of fact, I do have it here and was considering where to put it. Would you like to assist me?"

"Absolutely!" exclaimed Caitlin.

"Hey, he asked me," said Sam.

Caitlin sighed. "I meant us, Sam. Relax."

"Sam's hypersensitive about the vase," explained

Derek. "He thinks you're going to name it after him or something."

Patrick laughed. "That's perfectly understandable, Sam. It's pretty exciting to find an artifact like that. Come on. Let's go take a look."

They followed Patrick to a roped-off section toward the rear of the museum next to three tall windows. It was closed to the public, but Patrick unhooked the rope and let them walk through. "Be careful not to bump into anything," he warned. "It's still a bit of a mess."

"What is this display going to be about?" asked Caitlin.

"It's a focus on Persian ceramics, similar to the kind that Sam discovered. Most aren't as complete, however."

Sam looked around the small corner. Several opened wooden crates sat on the floor, overflowing with packing material. A six-foot display wall with glass shelves was partially filled with different kinds of pottery. The front of the case had a glass door, but Patrick opened it with a key.

"Where's my piece?" asked Sam expectantly.

"The museum's piece," Derek corrected him again.

Sam rolled his eyes but didn't say anything.

Patrick kneeled next to one of the wooden crates, pulling on a pair of white gloves. He reached into the crate, removing the top layer of packing material to reveal the front side of a shimmering brown and blue vase.

"Wow!" said Sam.

"It's so beautiful," marveled Caitlin.

"It's...it's...a Sam!" said Derek in a mocking tone.

"It looks a bit better than it did coming out of the ground, doesn't it?" asked Patrick, smiling. He slowly lifted the vase from the crate, holding it carefully in front of him for the kids to see.

Sam took a small step forward, but not too close. He didn't trust himself not to bump into it or trip over a crate and knock over the entire display. That would not be good. "It's so cool."

"Let's get it into the case so that we can see it better," said Patrick, placing it onto the middle of the glass shelf that was directly at Sam's eye level.

"Patrick, could you come to the front for a moment?" a voice from the radio on Patrick's belt squawked. He stood and closed the door to the display case, locking it with the key. "Can you guys stand guard here for a few minutes? I'll be right back."

"Sure," said Caitlin.

As Patrick walked away, Derek pushed Sam aside to stand in front of the case. "Very cool."

"Hey," said Sam, "move it." He shoved his brother back out of the way.

"Easy, guys," said Caitlin. "You're going to break something."

"You're right," said Derek, stepping back. "I don't want to accidentally break the *Sam*."

Sam ignored him and put his nose right up against the glass, staring at his vase. He liked how the sunlight streaming through the windows highlighted the blue in the pattern. He looked for the sparkling waves that he'd picked out when he'd seen it in the ground and then again in the lab, but he didn't see them. He leaned to the right for a different angle, but still couldn't see anything sparkling. "That's weird," he muttered.

"What's weird?" asked Caitlin, moving next to him.

"*Sam* is weird," said Derek. "I'll agree with that."

"The sparkles," said Sam, still staring through the glass. "Earlier, I picked out these tiny, blue, sparkling swirl patterns. They were really cool. But now I don't see them at all."

"Maybe they're on the other side," suggested Caitlin.

"Maybe, but I could swear they were on both sides." He stood back and looked at Caitlin. "Do you think they could have come off in the cleaning process?"

"I wouldn't think so." Caitlin put her hand on her chin, thinking. "If anything, you'd think the artifacts would be *more* sparkly than they were before the cleaning, but I don't really know. You should ask Patrick."

"We need to go find those bikes," said Derek behind them, growing restless. "We still have an assignment to do for the professor, remember?"

"He's right," said Caitlin. "We'll figure this out later."

"I guess..." said Sam, feeling disappointed. The sparkle swirls were his favorite part of the piece. It was still beautiful, but something wasn't sitting right about it in his mind. He just couldn't place it. "What about Patrick?" Sam looked down the aisle but didn't see him returning yet.

"He'll be back soon. This stuff is all roped off. It will be fine," said Derek, already moving down the hall toward the back door. "Last one to the bikes has to walk to the Settlement!"

Sam reluctantly turned and followed. He looked over his shoulder at his vase. "I'll be back," he said softly.

# CHAPTER THIRTEEN

They found the green shed next to a tree so wide and tall it looked to have been there since the time of the colonists. Derek opened the shed door with a loud creak, the light streaming into the dark room filled with dirt and cobwebs.

"What a mess," said Derek, coughing in the dusty air.

"Do you see any bikes?" asked Caitlin.

"Over here." Derek reached against the wall and wheeled a bicycle out into the sunlight.

Sam reached for a pair of handlebars. He pulled the bike toward him, then groaned.

"What's wrong?" asked Caitlin.

Sam pointed to the bike he'd pulled out. "Notice anything unusual?" The only bike left was one of those two-person, tandem bikes like he'd seen families riding together at the beach.

"Looks fine to me," said Derek. He hopped on his single bike and rode off before they could protest.

Sam glanced over at Caitlin. "Well..."

She smiled and grabbed the handlebars. "It'll be fine. Come on." She hopped onto the front seat and giggled. "Just don't make us crash!"

Sam shook his head and sat on the seat behind her. He grasped his handlebars uncertainly as Caitlin pushed off and they both began peddling. "This is crazy," he shouted, concentrating on his balance as the bike wobbled unevenly down the trail.

"You two coming?" Derek called, waiting for them just past the parking lot.

"Don't let him get to you," Caitlin said over her shoulder. "This is fun!"

As they started to move faster, Sam tried to keep the bike from getting too wobbly. "I don't think bikes were made to work like this," he said.

"We just have to work together," said Caitlin as they caught up with Derek.

Sam shot a nasty look at Derek as they rode past. He tried to think of something else. "So, what did the paper say on the professor's desk?" he called forward to Caitlin.

"It was a letter from the Smithsonian. It claimed that one of the artifacts from the dig site failed their authentication test."

Sam scrunched his eyebrows. "Their *what* test?"

"It means it was a fake."

"Fake?" said Sam. "You mean the artifacts aren't real?"

"That's what the letter said."

"But how could that be?" Sam thought about the thousands of items in the Archaearium that had been discovered at Jamestown. "I mean, we know they dug those things right out of the ground. I just did it myself this week."

"I don't know," said Caitlin. "But that must have been what the professor was arguing about on the phone."

"No wonder he sounded mad," said Sam. "I'd be really upset if someone said my vase was fake."

"The letter said that the Smithsonian was considering pulling their funding from the dig site if they didn't get an explanation."

"That's not good."

"It's terrible. Without funding, how are they supposed to continue discovering new things about our country's beginnings? I feel so bad for him. I wish we could help. "

"How would we do that?" asked Sam. He didn't want to sound stupid, but he really didn't have a clue about what they could do.

"I don't know yet," replied Caitlin.

Sam thought back to his vase in the display case and the swirling sparkles. Why were they missing? Could his vase be a fake too? That couldn't be possible. He'd pulled it from the ground himself.

"Hey, look!" said Caitlin.

Sam snapped out of his thoughts, hitting his brakes a little too hard. They swerved and skidded to a bouncy stop. "Whoa," he said, clutching his handlebars tightly. He turned in the direction that Caitlin was looking. "What is it?"

"The Glasshouse." She pointed to a small trail leading into the woods toward the water. "Let's go see it."

He'd been wanting to go there. He supposed now was a good time, if they didn't take too long. He tried to peddle forward, but the bike began to wobble harder and they nearly fell over.

Caitlin laughed as they struggled to balance themselves. "Maybe we should just walk there."

Sam slid his leg over his seat. "That's the best idea you've had all day."

They rested their bike next to a tree that was just off the road, then followed the path into the woods toward some buildings, waiting for Derek to follow them.

"I still don't understand what a glasshouse is," said Sam. Grace had said it was where they made glass, but that seemed strange.

"We're about to find out," answered Caitlin.

They walked into a wooden building that had a chimney jutting from the center of the sharply sloped roof. In the middle of the room, a man and a woman worked around a strange-looking structure. It was rounded, about ten feet across and the same amount wide. It looked like a small cave made out of cement and small rocks.

"What is it?" asked Sam.

"I think it's a furnace," said Caitlin, "but I don't know how it works."

"Whoa," said Derek, stepping next to them. "It's like a giant oven."

"That's exactly what it is," said the woman in front of them. She was dressed in a baggy white shirt, green pants that came down just below her knees, and white tights.

"How exactly do you make glass?" asked Sam, leaning against the railing that separated them from the oven and the workers.

"You blow it," answered the woman, whose name tag said *Mariana*.

"Blow it?" asked Derek. "What, like bubble gum?"

"Not exactly," Mariana said. "Let me show you." She walked up to the furnace where several long metal poles were sticking out from the flame.

"That looks hot," said Caitlin.

"Over two thousand degrees," Mariana answered.

Sam instinctively took a step backward. "Holy cow. That's really hot." He gulped, imagining how it would feel to be near that furnace. You'd probably be dead before you even reached the flames.

"Hot enough to melt glass," Mariana explained. She pulled a pole from one side of the furnace, then dunked it with a sizzle into a bucket of water on the ground. Then she placed it into another opening in the furnace, rolling the metal rod back and forth in her hands.

"First we dip our blowpipe into the furnace to gather a mixture of molten glass. Early settlers used a mix of ash, sand, crushed oyster shells, and burned seaweed. They'd heat it up in a furnace much like this one. Back then, it took many loads of wood to keep things burning this hot, but today we use natural gas."

They watched, entranced, as she gradually pulled the rod from the orange flames of the furnace. "Once it's properly heated, you have a ball of molten glass like this one." A glowing round glob that looked like lava was stuck to the end of her pole.

"That's glass?" asked Derek.

Mariana nodded. "Melted glass." She placed the lava ball into a steel cup and rolled it slowly on the pole, then moved it to a metal counter surface, gradually moving it back and forth until it formed a cylinder shape.

"That still doesn't look like glass," said Derek skeptically.

Mariana smiled, evidently used to impatient kids like

Derek doubting her craftsmanship. "Just wait, because here comes the magic part."

Sam's eyes widened as she raised the metal rod into the air, then, incredibly, placed her mouth to the end without the lava. She slowly blew into the rod, which Sam realized was a hollow tube, and the molten form on the far end began to puff out into a ball-like shape. It *was* almost like blowing a bubble.

"What does that do?" Sam asked.

"Blowing through the pipe makes the glass hollow," Mariana answered, lowering the rod onto a rack where she blew into the pole again before forming it further with a pair of metal tongs. What had been a glowing orange ball now looked more like a bright orange light bulb on the end of the metal pole.

Caitlin turned and smiled at Sam. "Isn't it so cool?"

"Hot, actually," joked Derek.

Sam nodded as Mariana repeated the process of blowing, turning the pole, and working with the tools to gradually mold it into the shape she desired. "What's it going to be?" he asked, finally.

"A small flower vase." She nodded behind them to another room. "There's a wide assortment of glassware in the store behind you. We've made it all right here from the kiln."

Sam couldn't seem to stop watching Mariana working with the glass. He'd never seen anything like that before.

But when Derek nudged him and signaled that they needed to go, he reluctantly stepped back from the railing.

"Thanks for showing us," Sam called. He stopped short of the doorway and turned back to Mariana. "Do you ever make pottery here too?"

"Not much," she replied. "But we do have a pottery wheel and a small kiln in the back where you could fire some ceramics if you wanted to. I haven't seen it used for a while though." She looked at him closely. "A hobby of yours?"

Sam blushed and shook his head. "No, just wondering. Thanks."

"You're welcome," answered Mariana. "Enjoy your time here at Jamestown."

"Don't worry," said Sam, turning to join Caitlin and Derek. "We will."

He followed them into the room that was filled with rows and rows of glass objects. There were cups and mugs, vases and pitchers, all in different colors of green, blue, and reddish brown.

"This is amazing," said Caitlin. "I can't believe all this was made in that oven back there."

"I never knew you could blow glass like that," said Derek. He looked over at Sam. "We should get one of these for Mom and Dad before we leave."

"Good idea," agreed Sam.

"But we still need to get over to the Settlement like the professor asked us to," reminded Caitlin.

"She's right," said Derek. "They might be wondering where we are."

"What were you asking Mariana, Sam?" said Caitlin.

He bit his bottom lip, not sure how to say what was circling in his mind. "She said that they have another kiln that can be used to make pottery."

"That sounds fun," said Caitlin. "I've always wanted to try that."

"Uh-huh," said Sam.

# CHAPTER FOURTEEN

W hen they got all their bikes moving again in the right direction, they rode across the narrow stretch of land that connected Jamestown Island to the mainland. They came to the large parking lot with the flags out front that they'd seen with Toby and Grace on their first day.

Caitlin pointed at the building. "This is Jamestown Settlement, so that must be the museum."

"I wonder why it's so much bigger than the dig site and the aquarium," said Derek.

"*Archaearium*, dummy," corrected Sam.

"Right, what did I say?"

"You said *aquarium*. That's for fish."

"Well, some of the artifacts there could be of fish," said Derek. "Or fish bones. It's an Archaearium Aquarium."

Sam shook his head. "Forget it."

"I think Grace said they've only been digging for the fort for twenty years," said Caitlin. "Maybe this building has been here longer."

"Maybe," said Sam. "Let's go in."

They entered an expansive lobby with a long counter and several ticket-buying windows. Sam puzzled over where they should go, but Derek stepped up to one of ticket windows and smiled at an old lady with gray hair. Her name tag said *Jean*.

"Hi there, Jean," said Derek with a smile. "How are you today?"

The woman looked up from her computer and smiled back, seeming a bit surprised. "I'm very well. Thank you for asking, young man. How may I help you?"

"We're looking for someone named Jada," said Derek. "Professor Evanshade asked us to meet with her. We're part of the Field School over on the island. Do you know where we can find her?"

Jean eyed them skeptically. "You three are a little young to be part of Field School, aren't you?"

Caitlin stepped up to the counter next to Derek. "We are, but we're old friends of the professor and he invited us to come."

"We're experienced investigators," said Derek confidently.

Sam rolled his eyes. His brother was nothing if not confident.

"Is that right?" said Jean, smiling. "Well then, let me see what I can do about tracking down Jada." She picked up a phone and spoke softly to someone on the other end. A few moments later, she hung up and looked back at them. "Jada is in the middle of a tour right now, but she asked for the three of you to make your way through the museum and she'll be with you when she's finished." She glanced over her shoulder. "Have you visited the Indian village, the fort, or the ships yet?"

They all shook their heads.

"Well that should keep you busy for a good while," said Jean. "Since you're part of Field School, you can come right in. No charge." She stood and opened a gate beside her window.

"Awesome," said Derek. "Thanks a million, Jean."

She smiled and waved them through. "My pleasure. I'll let Jada know where you are so she can track you down."

"Thanks," said Sam.

"Should we go through the museum first?" asked Caitlin, "Or go straight to the Indian village and the other stuff?"

Derek grinned. "What do you think?" He pushed open the door and charged outside. "To the fort, everyone!"

Caitlin turned to Sam with an annoyed glance. "Really?"

"Come on, we've seen plenty of museums. I want to see the fort and the ships too."

Caitlin shrugged as they followed Derek down the path into the woods. Soon they neared several small buildings, huts with thick, thatched, rounded tops.

"This must be the Indian village," said Sam.

"Let's check it out," called Derek, stooping slightly to enter the low door of the first hut.

While Caitlin looked at the basket-weaving display outside, Sam followed Derek into the hut. Animal skins were pinned to the inside walls and strewn across benches around the sides of the room. It was like a big camping tent, although it would be pretty scary to wake up in a tent with wild animal hides all around you. Sam thought he might have bad dreams for a month if he did that! A hole in the center of the roof was directly above a small fire pit on the ground.

Derek picked up a badger skin and draped it over his head. "Watch this," he said with a mischievous smile. "Hey, Caitlin, come in here!" He moved against the wall, nearly blending in with all the other skins like camouflage.

Sam shook his head as he saw Caitlin coming, but chuckled at the same time, wanting to see what she'd do.

"Cool!" She ducked through the doorway and looked around the room. "Where's Derek?"

Sam tried to keep a straight face as one of the skins on the wall began to move. Derek slowly crept up behind her with his arms out wide.

"Oooga Booga!" he yelled, grabbing her shoulders.

"Ahh!" screamed Caitlin at the top of her lungs. She spun around and karate kicked Derek in the chest, dropping him to the floor next to the fire circle.

Sam stared in shock at his brother buried in badger skins on the ground. He looked over at Caitlin, unsure whether to laugh or worry.

"Oh my gosh! Derek?" she exclaimed, bending down. "Are you okay?"

Derek rolled onto his back and moaned. "What the heck, Caitlin?"

"Why did you jump out at me like that?" asked Caitlin. "You scared me to death."

"Where did you learn to kick like that?" said Sam, still marveling at what had just happened. He'd never seen Derek take such a hit. He secretly wished it had been him, but having it come from a girl like Caitlin was just as good.

Caitlin frowned. "I'm sorry. I acted on instinct. I thought an animal was attacking me. I took martial arts for a few years with my dad."

"Way to go, tough guy," laughed Sam.

Derek sat up with a crooked grin on his face. "It seemed funnier in my mind."

"And don't act like the Indians were some dumb savages," said Caitlin. "They had very advanced cultures. They were the original settlers here, you know."

"Derek doesn't know a lot about advanced culture," said Sam. He turned toward the door. "Why don't we go to the fort? I think it might not be quite as dangerous."

"This time, I'll go first," said Caitlin, stooping back through the doorway.

Sam glanced back at Derek. He still seemed a bit dazed from the kick. "You okay?"

Derek nodded slowly. "Note to self. Don't scare Caitlin."

They walked past more Indian houses, a canoe carved from a tree trunk, and several other stations that showed how Indian tribes cooked, used shells for tools, and gardened.

"Look, there's the fort!" said Sam, walking faster.

"It's not the real fort, you know," said Caitlin.

"It's not?" asked Derek, as they entered through a gate in the perimeter wall, which had been made of vertical logs that were cut like sharp pencil points. "It looks pretty real to me."

"That's not what I mean," replied Caitlin. "It's a replica. The actual Jamestown fort was the one over at the dig site on the island."

"Then what's this one for?" asked Sam, looking around at the buildings. There were close to a dozen houses inside the triangle-shaped walls that protected the fort. He noticed platforms on the corner of the walls where soldiers could stand guard. These walls seemed much stronger than the ones on the island. One building was clearly a church, while another looked like a black-smith's.

"This is to show what the fort probably looked like when the colonists were here," said Caitlin. "I think so, at least. I don't know everything, you guys."

"You don't?" said Derek, dripping with sarcasm.

"Look over there." Sam pointed to one of the areas next to the wall. "What's that guy doing?"

"He's dressed like a soldier," said Derek.

They walked toward the man who was surrounded by several other visitors. He held a long rifle that he called a match-lock musket and demonstrated how to shoot. He first poured black powder into the gun, then stuffed a paper wad instead of a real lead musket ball into the gun with a long stick. He lit a short rope and set it on top of the firing mechanism.

"Present your piece!" he yelled, pressing the butt of the gun against his shoulder. "Give fire!" He squeezed the trigger, which moved the lit rope to the powder, setting off an explosion with a sharp bang.

Sam covered his ears. "That was loud!" he shouted.

"Can I try?" Derek asked the man, who grinned but shook his head.

After exploring the different buildings inside the fort, they turned back down the path toward the water. "Do you think they can actually sail these ships?" asked Sam.

"I don't know," said Caitlin.

"See, Caitlin, there's another thing you don't know," laughed Derek.

"Yeah, yeah," she answered, grinning.

They walked out to a wide dock where three wooden ships were tied to metal cleats with thick ropes. All three had tall masts with extensive rigging and turrets. The side of the largest boat was painted with bright blue and red designs.

Derek walked up to one of the informational signs. "I'll bet you can't tell me the names of the ships." He covered part of it with his hands. "Don't look."

"Wait, I know this one," said Sam. He thought for a moment. "The *Niña, Pinta,* and *Santa Maria*. Right?"

Caitlin laughed. "Nice try, Sam. I think those were Christopher Columbus's ships. These three are the *Susan Constant, Godspeed,* and the...wait, I know it, don't tell me."

"Mm-hmm," said Derek. "Sure you do."

"Wait, I do." She placed her hand on her head, concentrating. "*Susan Constant, Godspeed,* and the...*Discovery*! The *Discovery*! That's it, right?"

Derek stretched his lips into a flat smile, shaking his head. "No. I'm sorry, Caitlin. That is incorrect."

"What?" Caitlin exclaimed. "It *is* the *Discovery*."

"The correct answer is the *Sea Turtle*."

Sam burst out laughing. Derek usually gave him a hard time; it was fun to see him dishing it out to someone else for a change.

"The *Sea Turtle*!" said Caitlin. "You're crazy." She marched up to the sign, pushing Derek's arm out of the way. "See, right there, the *Discovery*."

"But originally it was named *Sea Turtle*," added Derek. "Doc told me that yesterday."

"Uh-huh," said Caitlin. "Nice try." She moved past him and onto an inclined metal ramp leading up into the largest of the boats.

"You'd better watch your back, Derek," Sam teased. "She might knock you down again." He made a karate chop motion and cracked up laughing as he boarded the boat.

"All aboard the *Sea Turtle*!" Derek shouted across the docks.

"This is the *Susan Constant*, dummy," said Sam.

"I knew that," said Derek.

# CHAPTER FIFTEEN

U p on the deck, they ran into a tour group moving down a narrow set of steps into the belly of the ship. A woman was leading them, calling out various facts as they walked.

"Let's follow them," said Derek. "I want to see what's down there."

They waited their turn, then carefully stepped down the steep, ladder-like boards. Sam looked around the cramped quarters inside the ship. The ceiling was low, and the room was filled with barrels and crates. Short, cot-like beds were scattered along the walls. He imagined trying to sleep inside the ship for a night. Did travelers back then get seasick? Months at a time stuck on a boat crossing the ocean must have been terrible.

"Sailors tracked the speed of the ship using a unit of

measurement called knots," the tour guide was saying to the people huddled around her.

"Knots?" asked one of the kids in the tour. "What's that?"

Sam noticed the leader's name tag. He nudged Caitlin. "Look, it's Jada!"

"Cool, let's listen," she replied.

"A knot is a measurement of speed on the water," Jada explained.

"That's a weird name," muttered Derek. "A knot is what I get in my shoelaces."

Jada must have heard him, since she smiled in his direction. "It might seem like an odd name, my friend, but if you know the context, it makes complete sense."

Sam's teachers were always talking about context in school. He wondered if Jada used to be a teacher or maybe she still was when she wasn't giving tours. He leaned around the man standing in front of him to see Jada holding a wooden board about the size of a Ping-Pong paddle.

"The crew on the *Susan Constant*, like other sailors of the early 1600s, used a device like this one."

"What's that?" someone else asked.

"It's called a log line." Jada held it higher to reveal how it was connected to a rope with markings on it. "While the ship was moving, a sailor would throw the wooden board into the water. He would count the length of rope that fed out into the water as the ship moved by the number of actual knots in the rope that passed through his hands. An hourglass was used as a timer. So, for example, if ten knots of the rope went into the water, the ship was said to be traveling a speed of ten knots."

"Wow," said Sam. He'd heard people talk about a boat going a certain number of knots, but he never knew that was what it meant.

"That's *not* what I expected." Derek laughed at his own lame joke.

When Jada dismissed the tour group to explore the rest of the ship, Caitlin walked up and introduced herself.

"Well, hello," said Jada pleasantly. "I'm glad you found me. What do you think of the ship?"

"It's fascinating," Caitlin said.

"Pretty cramped though," added Sam.

"Yes, it is. But if you wanted to cross the Atlantic back in the 1600s, this was the best method of transportation you had."

"I'm glad I didn't live back then," Sam replied.

"Me too," laughed Jada. "How 'bout we go above deck and get some fresh air?"

"Sounds good," said Sam, feeling a bit claustrophobic down below.

"The professor said you have an assignment for us?" asked Caitlin once they were back up in the sunlight. She seemed a little overeager as far as Sam was concerned. He wanted to know what they were there to do too, but it seemed like Caitlin was back in school, ready to write down everything the teacher said. She'd loosened up a lot from when they'd first met in third grade, but she still loved to learn and be the best at things.

"I do have an assignment for you," Jada replied. She winked at them. "Do you think you're up to it?"

"Absolutely," said Caitlin.

"Depends on what the assignment is, I guess," said Sam.

Caitlin frowned at Sam's response.

"I'm pretty sure you need Sam to clean toilets. Is that right?" said Derek.

Sam shot him a glare.

"No, we wouldn't make y'all do that," Jada chuckled, her hands on her hips. "Well, you've seen how I lead tour groups like the one on the ship. We also have a lot of children's programs. One of their favorite things is our colonial play, in which we just so happen to have several open key roles today."

"A play?" asked Sam, his eyes opening wide. "Like in a theater?"

Jada nodded. "Sort of, just not in an actual theater. We put it on outside here near the Indian village. Today we're missing the three lead actors for our Pocahontas play."

Derek grinned. "Sam would be perfect for Pocahontas!"

Sam slugged his brother in the arm. "Shut up, will you?"

Jada shook her head. "Now, now. I think Caitlin might make a better Pocahontas. What do you think?"

Caitlin's eyes lit up. "Oh, that sounds like so much fun!"

"Derek, do you feel like being Captain John Smith?" asked Jada.

"Do I get to carry a sword?"

Jada laughed. "Yes, but not a real one."

"Okay, I can do that." He pretended to slash at the air with his arm.

"Captain Smith is believed to have befriended a young Pocahontas in the first year at Jamestown," explained Jada. "She helped him with her people's language, food, and establishing trade. Smith was a terrific leader and explorer, but he was injured in a gunpowder explosion before their second winter and soon left the colony for England, never to return to Virginia."

"What about me?" asked Sam uncertainly. It seemed like Pocahontas and Captain John Smith were the two main parts. Maybe that was for the best. Derek pretended like he was on stage most of the time anyhow, and Sam had never been overly confident in front of a large group of people.

"Sam," Jada relied, "I think you'd make a great John Rolfe. What do you think?"

He looked at her suspiciously. "Um, what does John Rolfe do?"

"Well, John Rolfe was a very important settler at Jamestown and had a lot to do with the establishment of the colony. He was a tobacco planter and businessman. After narrowly surviving a shipwreck in Bermuda, he came to Jamestown with the supply ships that saved the colony from starvation."

That sounded pretty cool. He didn't mind being the guy who started a business and helped save the settlers. Maybe this wouldn't be so bad. "I guess I can do that."

"But," continued Jada, "he's most famously known for what happened in the first Jamestown church. You probably saw where it's been excavated inside the fort on the island."

"Oh yeah," said Sam. "That's what the 'X' stands for on the map of the fort." He wanted to get one of those hats like Toby had, with the fort drawing in the middle.

"What happened at the church?" asked Caitlin.

"Several years after Captain Smith returned to England, Pocahontas was kidnapped by English settlers and held for ransom."

"Kidnapped?" asked Caitlin. "Poor girl."

Jada nodded. "She ended up staying with the colonists, converting to Christianity, and changing her name to Rebecca."

"So what does all that have to do with John Rolfe?" asked Sam, trying to follow along.

"I'm getting there," said Jada. "John Rolfe had lost his wife and child during the time in Bermuda. A year after Pocahontas's baptism, she and John Rolfe were married. That's the highlight of our play today!"

Derek burst out laughing and pointed at Sam's face. "Ha! Sam and Caitlin have to get married!"

Sam felt his face grow bright red.

Caitlin waved Derek away and looked down at the ground. "Don't listen to him, Sam. It's just a play."

Sam put his hand over his face. He knew this was a going to be a bad idea.

"Oh, come on now, you guys," chided Jada. "Keep it together. The play is short, and the kids will really enjoy it." She motioned toward the museum. "Doc told me you three were used to challenges, no? Well think of this as a new kind of adventure." She turned to leave the ship. "Come on, let's go get your costumes."

"Costumes?" moaned Sam, starting to feel ill.

"Well, of course," said Jada. "You can't have a historical play without costumes, now can you?"

Sam shook his head as he followed behind them to the museum. "This is going to be a disaster."

# CHAPTER SIXTEEN

"I'm not coming out."

"Oh, come on, Sam," said Derek from the hall-way. "You're probably wearing the same thing I am. It's not so bad."

Sam looked at himself in the mirror. The costume Jada had given him seemed ridiculous. He couldn't believe the settlers of the New World could possibly have worn these kinds of clothes. He had high, white socks that came up over his knees, black leather shoes with a square buckle, baggy red pants that seemed ten sizes too big, and a matching red long-sleeved shirt that fitted tightly against his neck. To top it off, the droopy black hat he was supposed to wear seemed more like Donald Duck than Indiana Jones. He let out a long sigh and opened the door to the hallway.

Derek held back a laugh when he saw Sam step out of

the bathroom, but since he was dressed similarly, he kept a straight face. He had some sort of cape draped around his shoulders, but like Sam's clothes, it was kind of weird, and didn't remind him at all of anyone cool, like Superman.

"Whose idea was this again?" Sam said grumpily.

Derek shrugged his shoulders. "All part of the deal, I guess. Where's Caitlin?"

Before he could answer, another door opened from the hallway and Caitlin stepped toward them. "Well… what do you think?"

"Wow, you look great!" said Derek. He nodded at Sam, who still hadn't said anything. "Right, Sam?"

"Uh, yeah," Sam finally replied. He'd done a double take, but not because she looked bad. He couldn't help but notice that Caitlin looked very pretty, but her costume wasn't what he'd been expecting. She was in a colonial-style, blue and white dress with a poofy skirt, sleeves that came down to her wrists, and a bright red sash. "I thought you'd be wearing an Indian costume."

Caitlin nodded. "I know. I was surprised too, but Jada said that since we're reenacting the wedding, Pocahontas would be wearing English clothes instead of her traditional Powhatan dress."

"Huh," said Derek. "Who knew?"

"Look at you three!" exclaimed Jada, walking down

the hall behind them. "You look fabulous." She handed them each a small binder.

"What's this?" asked Sam.

"Your script, of course."

"We don't have to memorize it, do we?" asked Derek. "I perform best when I can improvise." He flashed a cheesy grin.

"No, you don't have to memorize it," said Jada. "But let's try to stick to the script today, okay? We don't need to start revising history for the kids."

Sam was wondering if he could revise his decision to be in this play. Digging for artifacts with Toby had been a lot more fun than dressing up in this clown suit. His arms were itching and he already felt sweaty, despite the air-conditioned hallway.

THEY HAD JUST ABOUT MADE it through the script, and much to Sam's surprise, it was kind of fun. Well, it wasn't exactly what he'd choose to do on a normal day, but it wasn't as bad as he'd expected. The worst part was the costumes. He couldn't imagine how the explorers wandered through the forests in those clothes. He hoped for their sakes they had more comfortable clothes for normal days.

It was fun watching the faces of the little kids in the

audience as they performed the play. Sam had never been in a play before; the most he had done was reading aloud in class. At home, he often felt like he must be on a hidden camera TV show because of the way Derek always carried on, but so far no one had shown him the footage.

Just as he and Caitlin moved toward the final wedding scene, thunder boomed overhead and rain began to pour down. The audience all scattered in a flurry, running with their families back to the museum.

"Ahh!" screamed Caitlin.

"Let's get out of here, Pocahontas!" called Sam.

"Follow me!" yelled Derek, just as another loud clap of thunder boomed through the clouds above them. He ran along the path toward the museum, but by the time they reached the Indian village, all three of them were soaked to the bone. Derek pointed through the rain to the Indian house they'd played in before, and they all squeezed through the low doorway.

"I'm drenched!" said Sam, trying to catch his breath. The clothes felt even more awkward when they were wet and weighing him down.

Caitlin collapsed next to him on the bench covered with animal hides. "That was crazy!"

"I guess we won't be able to do a curtain call," grumbled Derek.

Sam looked at him sideways. "You really liked that, didn't you?"

Derek nodded. "Yeah, it was awesome. Don't you think?"

"I liked it too. It was fun," Caitlin said.

"I suppose so," said Sam. He didn't think he'd be signing up for another play anytime soon, but he could easily believe that his brother enjoyed being the center of attention. Caitlin too, in her own way.

"What do we do now?" asked Caitlin.

"Wait for the rain to stop, I guess," said Derek.

Another loud boom of thunder shook the hut and Sam jumped. "That was close!"

"Don't worry. I'll protect you, Sam," said Caitlin, draping her arm around his shoulder.

He frowned and scooted away from her on the bench. He didn't like storms, but he didn't need Caitlin making fun of him either. He felt ridiculous enough in these clothes.

Derek peeked his head out the doorway of the hut. "The whole path is turning into a little river. If we get much more rain, we'll have to sail one of the ships out of here."

"You can take the *Sea Turtle*," said Sam.

"So why do you think the professor wanted us to do all this anyhow?" asked Caitlin, changing the subject.

"He said he got called away," replied Derek, "and I bet it has something to do with the letter from the Smithsonian and the fake artifacts."

The mention of the letter made Sam think about something Caitlin had mentioned earlier. "What did you say before about the fort and the ships?"

"That they were cool?" said Caitlin.

Sam shook his head. "No, you used a word when you described them."

"I did?"

"She uses a lot of words if you haven't noticed, Sam," said Derek.

"You said they weren't real..."

"Oh," remembered Caitlin. "Replicas. It means they're reproductions."

"Fakes?" asked Sam.

"Kind of," said Caitlin. "But not necessarily in a bad way. Why?"

"The letter, my vase, the ships..." Sam said slowly. He tried to verbalize what had been floating around in his mind. It was right there, but he couldn't quite see it.

"You want to put the letter in the vase on the ship?" asked Derek. "I think you got too much rainwater on your head, Sam. Or maybe that costume is too tight and cutting off the oxygen to your brain."

"Stop," said Sam, frowning. "Think about it. What do they all have in common?"

Caitlin's face brightened. "Wait, I see what you mean." She was quiet for a minute. "Are you thinking what I'm thinking?"

"Maybe." Sam stood and began pacing around the hut. "What if someone is purposefully making replicas of the artifacts from Jamestown, and then passing them off as real?"

"Why would they do that?" asked Derek.

"You heard what Toby said over at the dig site when Sam found the vase," said Caitlin. "These artifacts are priceless. They're worth a fortune."

"So, someone is selling them?" asked Derek.

"Maybe." Caitlin tipped her head to one side. "But what does that have to do with your vase, Sam?"

"Jamestown's vase," said Derek.

Sam shook his head; it didn't seem like his brother was going to let that one go. "The sparkles. They changed. I know it. They were the best part, but when I looked at it in the display case at the Archaearium, they were different."

"Maybe you misremembered them," said Derek.

Sam shook his head. "No, I'm sure." Then something clicked in his mind. "And I can prove it!"

"You can?" asked Caitlin. "How?"

Sam reached into his pocket for his phone, but once again, it wasn't there.

"What is it?" asked Caitlin.

"If I had my phone, I could show you the picture I took of the vase in the lab. It should show the sparkles."

"You didn't lose it again, did you, Sam?" chuckled Derek.

Sam glared at him. "No, I didn't lose it. It's in my other clothes back at the museum. We have to go back and get it."

"After it stops raining so hard," said Derek, looking out the doorway.

"Do you really think the professor's in trouble?" asked Sam.

"I hope not," answered Caitlin, "but if people believe he's been trying to pass off fakes as real artifacts, that could be really bad for Jamestown's reputation, not to mention his."

Sam shook his head. "He doesn't seem like someone who would do that." They'd known the professor ever since they'd brought him some stolen coins that Derek had found in a cave near their house. He always reminded Sam of a jolly old grandpa or the guy who made the dinosaurs in the *Jurassic Park* movie.

"Of course he isn't," said Caitlin. "That's why we have to help him."

"Easier said than done," said Derek.

"Well if it isn't the professor who's sending the fakes to the Smithsonian, that means someone else must be doing it," said Sam.

"Remember how Jerry was trying to steal the copy of

the Declaration of Independence behind the Wythe House?" said Derek. "It could be someone like him."

Sam shivered thinking about Jerry. They'd beaten him to the treasure on another adventure, and Jerry had not been happy about that.

"Maybe it *is* Jerry," suggested Derek, his eyes bugging.

Sam straightened up on the bench. "It *can't* be Jerry. He's in jail." He looked at Caitlin, trying to think. "Isn't he?"

She nodded. "I think so."

"But we don't know how long he was put away for, do we?" asked Derek. "Maybe he just got a stiff fine and now he's out on parole." He looked around the hut suspiciously. "Maybe he's watching us right now, plotting his revenge. Williamsburg isn't far from here, you know."

Sam didn't really know how the court systems worked, but he thought he remembered his dad explaining that criminals could get out early on parole if they'd behaved in jail. The only person he'd ever met who had been in prison before was Mad Dog DeWitt. He was the leader of the Confederate Ghosts biker gang that helped them on adventures on Belle Isle and at Swannanoa. But he wasn't anything like Jerry.

"I'm sure it's not Jerry," said Caitlin.

Sam tried to put the idea out of his mind. "Well, whoever it is, we have to get to the bottom of it."

"Agreed," said Derek.

A radio squawked outside the hut and they heard footsteps splashing in the puddles. Jada's face poked through in the doorway. "You kids okay in here?"

"Yeah, we're just trying to stay dry," answered Caitlin.

"Well, don't get too comfortable." Jada looked concerned. "Toby just radioed that they need your help right away over on the island. The storm has caused all kinds of problems with the dig site, and they need all the hands they can get."

"Oh, no!" exclaimed Caitlin.

"Let's go," said Derek, piling out of the hut behind Jada.

"Let me drive you," offered Jada. "It's quicker."

Sam looked down at his wet costume. "What about our clothes?"

"No time," said Derek.

"I'll hold your other clothes in my office," said Jada. "You can come back over to get them later."

Sam shrugged reluctantly as he raced behind Derek and Caitlin, jumping over puddles as they followed Jada to her car in the parking lot.

His phone would have to wait.

# CHAPTER SEVENTEEN

The rain had slowed considerably when Jada dropped them off at Historic Jamestown. Toby nearly bumped into them as he dashed into the parking lot.

"Where should we go?" called Derek to him.

"The West Wall," replied Toby over his shoulder. "The rain got through the protective tarps and the whole thing is flooded. I have to get more rope from my Jeep."

"Oh no," Caitlin said.

"Come on." Derek led the way.

They ran down the service road beside the Archaearium and the fort. Nearly all the tourists had left during the rainstorm, but many of the archeologists and other Jamestown staff were still scurrying about.

They hurried over to the West Wall, which wasn't easy in their bulky costumes. When they reached the dig holes, Sam stared in disbelief. Huge puddles filled nearly half of each of the squares. The blue tarps had sunk down into the holes, allowing buckets of storm water to flood the whole site. It was terrible.

"What a mess!" said Derek.

"How did this happen?" asked Caitlin, shaking her head.

Grace walked toward them, her face serious.

"Did the tarps not hold?" asked Sam.

"There's nothing wrong with the tarps," said Grace. "Someone untied them."

"Untied them," gasped Caitlin. "You mean, on purpose?"

Grace nodded. "Looks like it."

"Like sabotage?" asked Derek, his eyes perking up.

"Could be," answered Grace. "We've had some people tamper with things in the past out here, but they've never done anything this destructive."

Toby jogged up to where they were standing. He threw his hands out in disgust. "Unbelievable. This is going to set us back weeks!"

"Can't you just pump the water out of the holes?" asked Sam. It would be a lot of work, but he figured once the water was out, things would be all right.

Toby shook his head. "It's not that easy, I'm afraid. The dirt and mud has washed over all the spots we painstakingly uncovered. We'll have to be just as careful when we're brushing back the layers as we were before. We don't want to accidentally damage anything."

"I can't believe anyone would do something so stupid," Caitlin huffed. "Don't they know how important this is?"

Caitlin always got worked up over an injustice. It was one of the things Sam liked most about her. She didn't stand around and let people do bad things if she could help it. Mad or not, he wondered if there really was anything to be done this time.

"Look, it's the professor!" said Derek, pointing behind them.

Sam turned to see the professor walking slowly across the grass toward them. He was shaking his head and muttering to himself. "Just as I feared," he said as he reached the flooded area.

"It's a real mess, Doc," said Grace.

"Yes," the professor replied. "I heard the chatter on the radio." He held up his walkie-talkie from his pocket. "One more bad piece of news on a day that's already been filled with it."

"Why, what else is wrong?" asked Caitlin.

The professor sat down on the bench next to them and sighed. "I've just returned from an emergency meeting at the Smithsonian."

"In Washington, DC?" asked Derek.

The professor nodded. "That's right. It's less than

three hours away if traffic is on your side, which thankfully it was today. That's about the only good news I can report."

"What was the meeting about?" asked Caitlin.

Sam glanced up at Grace and Toby, who seemed anxious, looking uncomfortably at each other like they already knew what he was going to say.

"Well," said the professor, "I've been trying to keep the news from everyone the best I could, although I assume some of it has leaked out anyhow. But after today, there's really no use in holding back."

"What happened?" asked Caitlin.

"It seems one of the pieces from our collection that was shipped up to the Smithsonian has failed the authentication test. They're claiming that we've misrepresented our findings. Essentially, they're calling Jamestown a fraud."

"What?" exclaimed Derek.

"That's ridiculous, Doc," said Toby.

"Yeah, everybody knows that can't be true," said Sam.

"Surely they can't think that *everything* is a fake," said Caitlin. "Aren't there thousands of items that have been discovered here? All the treasures in the Archaearium?"

"Well, of course you're right. And I'm exaggerating a bit. They're not questioning the entirety of Jamestown, only the one piece is in doubt currently. But it calls into question our integrity. My integrity, certainly. And if this one item is deemed inauthentic, it raises doubts about what else we might be hiding."

"We're not hiding anything," growled Toby. "They should come out here to see for themselves what we've done. They should be thanking us."

"Yeah," said Sam. "What about the vase I just found? Are they questioning that, too?"

The professor smiled. "It's okay, everyone. We'll figure something out. But the long and the short of it is they've threatened to pull funding from the Jamestown Rediscovery project in thirty days if we can't get to the bottom of things." He shook his head slowly. "We receive such little federal funding as it is. Things will get very tight."

"What should we do?" asked Grace.

The professor let out a long breath, then looked up at them. "I'm afraid we have no choice but to suspend Field School for the rest of the summer."

"What?" said Toby. "Doc, how is that going to help anything?"

"I don't want to do it any more than you do, Toby," the professor replied. "But look around you. The West Wall dig alone is going to take weeks to dry out, not to mention the time it will take to get back to the soil layers we were at previously."

"There has to be an explanation," said Caitlin.

"I'm sure you're right, Caitlin," answered the

professor weakly, "but right now I don't know what it is. I'm going to have to convene an emergency meeting of the foundation's board of trustees. They'll want answers, and right now I'm not sure what to tell them. I need time to prepare."

Sam couldn't believe what he was hearing. How could they cancel Field School, or even worse, suspend their digging? What was going to happen to Jamestown?

The professor stood, turning toward the water. "All this time," he said softly, staring out into the distance, "Jamestown has been lying here in the ground, waiting to be discovered." He took several steps toward the river and they all followed, waiting to hear what he would say.

"Some evenings I walk here along the river, the cool breezes blowing across the water." He glanced up at the statue next to them. "I stand right here, in Captain Smith's shadow. Sometimes I even talk to him. Do you know what we talk about?"

"Swimming?" asked Derek.

Sam closed his eyes. His brother didn't know when to quit.

The professor chuckled. "No, Derek. I ask him how it felt four hundred years ago as one of the first English settlers on this shore. Each one of them with hopes, dreams, and fears. What it was like to struggle to survive, to adapt, to carry on despite so many hardships."

"Does he answer you?" asked Sam, trying to be serious.

"Sometimes." The professor smiled gently. "Sometimes he does, Sam." He spread his arms out wide. "This ground, this place, it's full of stories. Full of history, yes, but full of the lives of men and women who gave all they had. This ground is hallowed."

He turned and looked at them. "Did you know that when we started digging here, people said it was a fool's errand, that it couldn't be done?"

"They did?" asked Caitlin.

The professor nodded. "That's right. Most believed that the fort had been located on land that was now submerged, lost to the river."

"But you found it, Professor," said Grace. "You did it."

"We did it together, Grace. It was a team effort, and a monumental achievement, it's true." He took a long breath. "Toby, Grace, I'm going to need you for a few days to help straighten up the place. Kids, I want you to call your parents tonight and ask them to come and pick you up in the morning. I'm afraid there's no point in your staying."

"What?" cried Sam.

"But we want to stay, Professor," said Caitlin.

"Come on now, Doc!" said Derek. "You know we're

great at solving mysteries. We all know this can't be true, and we're going to help you get to the bottom of it."

The professor shook his head solemnly. "I'm afraid this might be one problem that is too big for even you kids to help solve."

# CHAPTER EIGHTEEN

"I can't believe this," said Sam, shaking his head as they walked back toward the building. He felt like he was in the middle of a bad dream, one where everyone wore weird clothing. He really needed to get out of his stupid play costume. They'd used Derek's phone to call home and tell Mom and Dad they had to be picked up in the morning.

"Did you do something wrong?" Mom had asked, knowing all too well that the boys often got tangled up in more trouble than they should. Derek had assured her it wasn't because of anything they'd done. He explained about the artifacts, and the Smithsonian, and the flooding. Sam was glad Derek was the one who called. He was feeling really sad about leaving Field School and didn't want to tear up on the phone in front of Caitlin and Derek.

Caitlin seemed more mad than sad when she called her parents. "It's not fair," Caitlin said when she finished her call. "There has to be a way to prove that they're lying."

"No one's really lying if they believe that the artifact was a reproduction," said Derek. "But I think Sam's right."

Sam raised his head. "You do?" He wasn't used to hearing that from his big brother.

Derek patted Sam on the head. "Just this once, Sam. Don't get used to it."

Sam brushed the hand away.

"Right about what?" said Caitlin.

"About the fakes," said Derek. "Someone has to be switching out the real artifacts for reproductions."

"Well, it's not the professor," said Sam.

"Yeah, I think we all agree on that," said Caitlin.

"Then who?" asked Sam.

"We should make a list," declared Caitlin.

"You always want to make a list," chuckled Sam.

"That's because they're always so helpful," Caitlin replied.

"Okay," said Derek. "So who are the possibilities?"

"I hate to say it, but I think it could be Grace," said Sam.

"No way!" Derek stood up with a hurt look on his face. "She couldn't...she wouldn't."

"Why not?" asked Caitlin.

"Because..." He paused like he was trying to think of a reason. "Because she's so cute, I guess."

"That's not a good reason," said Caitlin, rolling her eyes.

"Well, regardless, I still don't think it's her."

"Think about it," said Sam. "Remember how she was complaining about her student loans? It sounded like she owes a lot of money, which could be the reason that she needs to sell the artifacts."

Derek frowned and shook his head. "But how would she do it? I don't think she's around the artifacts that much, and it would take a lot of work to make a reproduction."

Sam nodded. "But didn't she say she was an art major? Maybe that could help her with the reproductions. And she was out here when we saw the figures in the church."

"Those are good points," said Caitlin, "but I think it's Marcus."

"Marcus?" asked Sam. "Why would it be him?"

"Well, unlike Grace, he has plenty of time with every artifact, working in the lab. You said it yourself—he's the one who cleans them when they come out of the ground. He could easily switch them out before sending them off to the museums. And he's an expert on all the different items."

"But why would he do that?" asked Derek. "Doesn't he like his job?"

"It seemed like he did to me," said Sam. "He was pretty strict, but I don't know if he'd steal the artifacts. He seemed nice."

"Being nice has nothing to do with it," said Caitlin.

"Jerry wasn't nice," said Sam, thinking back to their old nemesis from Church Hill.

"That's just one person," replied Caitlin. "And he probably did seem nice to other people, just not to us because we were hot on his trail."

"Well, I like that idea better than Grace," said Derek. "But it could also be Patrick."

"Patrick?" said Sam. "Why?"

"Don't you remember what happened when he gave us the ride to the island? He just disappeared while we were in the lab. Maybe he was one of the people in the shadows in the church and that's the reason we couldn't find him."

"Being in charge of the Archaearium displays, he would have plenty of opportunity to switch out the artifacts just like Marcus," agreed Caitlin. "And didn't you say you thought your vase seemed changed, Sam?"

Sam's eyes lit up. "That's right, my vase!" He'd almost forgotten about it with all the excitement from the storm and what the professor had told them.

"Jamestown's vase," Derek said again.

"Be quiet," said Sam. "I need to get to the picture on my phone. It could be proof that the vase is different."

"I thought you'd lost your phone again," said Derek.

"I didn't lose it," sighed Sam. "We just left it over at the Settlement museum with our regular clothes."

"We have to go change anyhow. Let's go do that now so we can get out of these horrible costumes," suggested Caitlin.

"Good plan, but we left our bikes over at the museum," moaned Sam.

"Maybe we can catch a ride." Derek pointed to someone walking out toward the parking lot. "Who's that?"

Sam strained his eyes to make out who the person was. "I think it's Grace."

"Perfect," said Derek. "I'll bet she can give us a ride."

Caitlin hesitated. "Can we trust her?"

"It's just a car ride," said Derek. "And we can't go accusing anyone without proof."

"I thought you said she was innocent?" said Sam.

"She is," said Derek. "I'm just saying, even if she wasn't, it's not like we have anything to worry about."

Sam tugged on the wet collar around his neck. "Okay, let's ask her. Anything to get out of this costume."

# CHAPTER NINETEEN

S am walked back into the hallway at the museum after dropping his costume off in Jada's office. He turned his neck in small circles, glad to be free of the wet, constricting clothes.

"Where's Caitlin?" asked Derek.

"I think she's still changing," said Sam. He didn't see the women's restroom in the hall and didn't know where Caitlin had actually gone. He opened his phone, happy to have it back, and sent her a quick text. Then he pulled up the picture of his vase and showed it to Derek.

"Look, do you see those sparkles on the blue swirls? I knew it!"

Derek stared at the phone. "We need to compare it to the vase in the display case."

"You know," said Sam. "I just thought of something."

"What?"

"What if they're all working together?"

"Who?" asked Derek.

"Grace, Marcus, and Patrick. What if they're all in a huge crime ring, working together to steal the artifacts?"

"That seems unlikely," said Derek. He glanced down the hallway. "Do you think Jean at the ticket counter is the ringleader too? And what about Jada?"

"That's not what I meant."

"Let's get over to the Archaearium and look at the vase before we add anyone to the suspect list."

"What about Caitlin?" asked Sam. He glanced at his phone. She still hadn't responded.

"I don't think she's a suspect," said Derek.

"No, I mean we can't leave her."

"Text her again and tell her to meet us there." Derek pushed through the side door to the parking lot.

"Are we walking?" asked Sam, following behind as he typed.

"We'll take the bikes," said Derek, pointing to where they'd left them earlier in the day.

"We need to leave one for Caitlin..." Shoot. That would mean he and Derek had to ride the tandem together.

Derek grabbed the double bike's front handlebars and pulled it onto the pavement. He grinned at Sam. "What, don't you trust me?"

Sam shook his head. "No. I don't trust you at all."

He'd had a hard enough time riding the crazy bike with Caitlin steering. He didn't want to think about how it might be with Derek driving.

"Come on," said Derek, climbing onto the seat. "What's the worst that could happen?"

Sam knew he had no choice. They had to get over to the Archaearium and look at the vase. They were running out of time. Whoever was switching the artifacts might know the professor was on high alert now that Field School was canceled. Whatever they were doing would surely be more difficult now that it had been detected.

Sam swung his leg over the bike and grasped the handlebars. "Just don't kill me, okay?"

"Hang on!" yelled Derek as they pushed off and wobbled for several feet until they got their momentum.

# CHAPTER TWENTY

Caitlin folded the sash and placed it neatly on top of the rest of her costume. She'd picked the oversized bathroom stall for extra room to change. She was about to open the stall door when she heard someone else enter the restroom. Something in the back of her mind told her to wait, so she stepped backward and listened. Someone was talking quietly on a phone.

"I know," the voice whispered. "The timing is terrible. What are we going to do?"

Caitlin froze as she recognized Grace's voice echoing faintly off the bathroom tiles. She didn't know what to do. Could Grace really be a suspect? Carefully, she climbed up onto the toilet, silently perching herself out of sight, her costume clutched tightly between her chest and her knees.

"There's just no time," Grace continued to whisper. She was pacing back and forth, and Caitlin held her breath each time the footsteps tapped close to her stall. She was trapped, but she didn't know what else to do besides listen. Maybe she could learn something. She hadn't really thought that Grace could be involved with the artifact switching, but now she was having second thoughts. What was she talking about?

"Do you think we still can?" Grace said. "But what about Doc? He might find out." There was a pause. "Okay, well if you think so. I had to bring the kids over to the Settlement museum, but I think I can get away without them noticing." She paused again. "Okay, I'll meet you at the Glasshouse in ten minutes. But make sure you're not followed."

Caitlin's cell phone suddenly buzzed in the pocket of her shorts. She gasped, not able to reach for it from her perch in the stall. Her hands were both full, and if she moved, Grace would hear her. She closed her eyes and hoped it didn't buzz again. She wondered if Grace had heard it from the other side of the bathroom.

The buzzing stopped, but now it was silent in the bathroom. Grace had stopped talking. Caitlin heard footsteps coming her way, then the sound of a stall door opening. Grace was checking the stalls!

Caitlin tried to remember how many stalls were in

the bathroom. Three, she thought, but she couldn't be sure. The footsteps stopped outside her stall. Grace pushed on the door, but it was locked. Caitlin's heart was beating so loud she was sure Grace could hear it too. A shadow formed under the door as Grace bent down to look for feet. The bottom of the sash hung down from the costume pile, and Caitlin pulled it up higher so nothing could be seen.

She didn't dare to breathe.

Finally, Grace's footsteps walked away from the stall. Caitlin heard the door to the bathroom open and close. She sat frozen for another minute just to make sure Grace hadn't pretended to leave or suddenly came back in, but all stayed quiet.

When she was sure Grace was gone, she climbed down to the floor, careful not to fall into the toilet. She stretched her legs, which had nearly gone numb from sitting in such an awkward position for so long. She unlocked the stall door and slowly pushed it open, scanning the room. It was empty. She looked at herself in the mirror over the sink. Her face was pale, like she'd seen a ghost. She set the pile of clothes on the counter and pulled out her phone.

It showed several texts from Sam.

*Where r u???*

*We're biking to Archaearium to compare my picture to the vase*

*We left you single bike, meet us there*

Caitlin frowned as she picked up her costume and walked to the door. She must have been hiding in the bathroom longer than she'd thought. Slowly, she stuck her head out and looked down the hallway. When the coast seemed clear, she scampered to Jada's office, set the clothes on the chair next to Sam and Derek's, and walked outside.

She wished they hadn't left her. She needed to tell them about Grace. It was nice of them to leave her the single bike, although she couldn't quite imagine them working together on the tandem bike without wiping out.

She kept an eye out for Grace, but she didn't feel as vulnerable now as she had in the bathroom, overhearing the phone conversation. She'd just play it cool if she ran into her out here. While she hadn't heard both sides of the conversation, it was pretty clear that Grace was plotting to meet someone. Was she handing over more stolen artifacts before the professor closed down Field School? Caitlin had to hurry.

She dialed Sam's number, but he didn't answer.

*Emergency!* she texted as she climbed onto the bicycle.

*It's Grace!*

*She's meeting someone at Glasshouse right now!*

*I'm following her. Meet me there.*

Caitlin pushed her phone back into her shorts pocket

just as a car passed on the other side of the parking lot. It was Grace. She was headed back to the island.

Caitlin pushed down on the pedal, staying along the edge of the parking lot to stay out of view. She had to get to the Glasshouse before it was too late!

# CHAPTER TWENTY-ONE

S am and Derek rode their bike right up to the front
entrance of the Archacarium. Sam wasn't sure how
they managed to do it without crashing, but it might
have had something to do with being focused on the
mission to discover the truth. Somehow, solving a
mystery was one of the few times that he and Derek
seemed to be able to work well together.

"Should we just march in?" asked Sam. "What if
Patrick is there? He might be the one doing the switching. If he catches on to what we're doing, he might get
dangerous."

"We're just going to have to risk it," answered Derek.
"There's no time to sneak around." He opened the door
and they walked into the lobby. "Besides, this shouldn't
take long. You just have to compare the picture to the
vase in the display case, right?"

"Right."

"Okay, then let's do it."

Despite Derek's plan, Sam still kept a lookout for Patrick. He truthfully didn't know if Patrick, Marcus, Grace, or maybe even someone they hadn't suspected was stealing the artifacts. Not knowing who to worry about made him nervous. When they'd tried to beat Jerry in the Church Hill mystery, at least they knew early on who they were dealing with.

They waved to the woman at the front desk and made a beeline to Sam's vase at the back of the museum. The display case now contained several other artifacts, but it was still roped off. Derek took a quick glance around and then slipped under the barrier and moved right up to the display case. Sam followed, his heart beating fast, worried that Patrick would come around the corner at any time. He knew they'd have a reasonable excuse, since Patrick already knew that Sam was interested in the vase. But if Patrick really was the culprit, there was no telling what he might do.

"Get your phone," whispered Derek.

Sam pulled up the picture he'd taken in the lab, enlarging the section that showed the sparkles. He held it as close to the glass door as he could. "See, look at the picture. Right there, near the middle. See those sparkles? Now look at the case. No sparkles. It's totally been switched."

Derek leaned, looking at the picture then back out at the display case. "I think you're right," he said finally, after comparing the two several times. "Those are definitely not the same. And you're sure this is the right vase?"

Sam frowned. "This is *my* vase, Derek. Or at least the one in the picture is. I dug it out of the ground. I'm not going to forget it."

"But how could they have copied it so closely?" asked Derek. "Someone would have had to make a whole new vase, paint it, or glaze it, or whatever you do to a vase, and then somehow try to make it look old again."

Sam nodded. It did seem like a big task. "I don't know how they did it, but that's the only explanation I can think of. Caitlin said they make reproductions of things like boats; maybe they can do it the same way with pottery."

Sam's phone buzzed in his hand. He turned it to see a text from Caitlin. His eyes opened wide and he showed the message to Derek.

"I don't believe it," said Derek, shaking his head. "It can't be Grace."

"Well I don't think Caitlin is going to make that up," said Sam. "There must be a reason that she's saying it's Grace. Either way, Caitlin's following her on the bike to the Glasshouse. We have to help her." He held his phone back up to the vase in the display case. "And now we have proof to show the professor!"

Sam turned and headed for the door. He wasn't going to wait for Derek to agree with him. He had the proof they needed, and Caitlin had discovered the culprit. He just hoped they could get to her before it was too late. Whatever Grace was involved in, it might be dangerous, and he didn't want to make Caitlin face it alone. Now he felt bad for leaving her back at the museum.

Sam sprinted through the lobby and out the front door. He rounded the corner to where they'd parked their bike, but nearly crashed into someone coming up the walkway. "Oh, sorry," cried Sam.

Marcus stood there surprised, carrying several bags in his hands. "Oh, Sam, where are you off to in such a big hurry?"

Sam's mind was racing with the new information and worry for Caitlin. "I have to get to the Glasshouse! Caitlin figured out that Grace has been stealing the artifacts and replacing them with replicas. I have proof right here on my phone with the picture of my vase."

Marcus raised his eyebrows at the news. "Are you sure about that?"

Sam nodded excitedly. "I took a picture in the lab, and the vase that's in the display case inside is not the same one as the lab. Grace switched the two of them just like the fake artifact at the Smithsonian! We're going to show it to the professor."

"You took a picture in the lab? My lab?" Marcus asked, his face looking like he'd just been stabbed in the heart.

Sam realized he shouldn't have said anything about the picture, since Marcus had told him not to take it, but the words were just spilling out of his mouth. The truth was too important, even though he had broken a rule. It was worth it now.

Derek came out the door behind them and continued over to their bike. "Come on, Sam. Let's go."

"Sorry about that, Marcus," said Sam, "but I gotta go. I'll tell you more after we save Caitlin and get the professor." He hurried over to Derek and the bike. They quickly pushed off and tore across the grass toward the Glasshouse.

# CHAPTER TWENTY-TWO

Caitlin peddled quickly up the road, keeping a lookout for Grace as she crossed the bridge onto Jamestown Island. The rain had ended, but thick clouds still filled the sky, making the early evening seem darker than usual. She slowed as she approached the sign for the Glasshouse, laying her bike under some bushes off the road. Tourist hours were over, so the island was mostly deserted aside from a few staff. But no one seemed to be out near the Glasshouse. She peered through the trees and saw a lone car in the parking lot. It was Grace's.

Caitlin jogged cautiously up the trail. She needed to get closer to see what Grace was up to. She hadn't planned what she would do when she got there, but they had to have proof if Grace was the one stealing the artifacts. The fate of the Jamestown Rediscovery project might depend on it!

She thought about why Grace would do such a thing. Her mom said you never really knew someone until you'd walked a mile in their shoes, which she assumed meant you had to see something from another person's point of view. Sure, she'd heard Grace's comment about her student loans. Maybe needing money really could motivate someone to commit a crime.

As she neared the Glasshouse, Caitlin paused behind an informational sign on wooden posts and listened. The Glasshouse was closed and all was quiet. She stepped forward into the open, watching for movement.

"Stop right there."

Caitlin froze. She turned slowly to see Grace standing behind her. She must have been hiding in the trees as Caitlin approached.

"Oh, hi, Grace," Caitlin said, trying to act normal. "What are you doing here?"

"I was just about to ask you the same thing."

Caitlin's mind flashed back to Jerry holding a revolver on them in the Wythe House. Grace didn't seem overly menacing; in fact, she seemed more nervous than anything.

Caitlin tried to think of a reasonable excuse. "I was just meeting Sam and Derek at the Glasshouse. We wanted to buy our parents gifts from the shop inside. Since we're leaving in the morning, we thought we'd better do it tonight." She attempted a weak smile, hoping that Grace believed her lie.

Grace nodded like she was going for it. "It's closed already, sorry."

"Oh, okay. Well, I can go back and wait for the boys by the road." Caitlin turned to step back up the trail. Spying on Grace was one thing, but she didn't want to be stuck without any backup. She hoped the boys had received her message.

"Hang on," said Grace, moving closer. "Are you following me?"

"What?"

"I said, are you following me? Were you in the bathroom at the museum?"

"Me?" Caitlin stuttered. "No, I told you. I was just—"

Grace closed her eyes. "You were! I knew I heard something." She let out a long sigh. "What are you doing here, Caitlin? You don't need to be in the middle of this."

Caitlin's heart was racing again. She had to find out more information. "In the middle of what?"

Grace just glanced at her watch nervously.

"Why would you do it, Grace?" Caitlin finally blurted out, unable to hold back any longer. "I thought you loved archaeology. How could you ruin everything for the professor? For Jamestown?" She couldn't decide if she felt like screaming or crying, but it was hard to hold back her emotions.

Grace looked confused. "Wait a minute, Caitlin. What are you talking about?"

"The artifacts. Why are you stealing them? They're priceless parts of our history!"

Grace's mouth opened wide in surprise. "You think I'm stealing the artifacts?" She seemed to put together what Caitlin was saying all at once. "That I'm behind the problems with the Smithsonian?"

Caitlin frowned. "You're not?"

Grace put her hand to her forehead with a pained look. "No, Caitlin. I'm not. I promise you that."

Caitlin's head was spinning. "Then what are you doing here?"

# CHAPTER TWENTY-THREE

"Look! Caitlin's bike," Sam said. They had reached the trail for the Glasshouse.

"Did she really say that Grace admitted to stealing the artifacts?" asked Derek as they came to a stop.

"Well, I don't know if she admitted it, but Caitlin said she's the one. Look, there's Grace's car!" Sam pointed at the parking lot as they slinked toward the building. "I hope Caitlin's all right."

As they moved closer, they heard talking and crouched down in the trail. "It's them!" Sam could see the two girls talking to each other. "We have to do something."

"Follow my lead," said Derek, standing up quickly. He strode toward the girls just in front of the Glasshouse. "There you are, Caitlin!" he said loudly. "The professor was looking for you."

Caitlin and Grace both startled at Derek's shout.

"Are you okay?" Sam asked Caitlin, following close behind.

She nodded, and then held her palm up. "It's okay, guys. Grace was just about to explain what's going on."

"I think there's been a misunderstanding," started Grace. "I'm not doing anything involving the artifacts." She turned back to Caitlin. "I think you thought you heard something in the restroom."

Caitlin looked skeptical. "You were talking to someone about running out of time and about the professor not finding out. If you're not stealing the artifacts, then what was all of that?"

Grace squirmed uncomfortably, looking up the path like she expected someone else to be coming. "Okay, but you guys have to promise not to say anything."

"That depends on what you're up to," said Sam.

"Yeah, we're not going to cover up some kind of crime against Jamestown, Grace," said Caitlin, hands on her hips. "That's not right."

"Why don't you just tell us," said Derek gently.

Sam crossed his arms suspiciously. He knew his brother never liked the idea that Grace could be the culprit, but they had to deal with the real facts.

Grace let out a deep breath. "Okay, so here's the thing. I *have* been taking something from Jamestown that I shouldn't have."

"I knew it!" snapped Sam.

Derek shook his head. "Let her finish, Sam."

"But it's not what you think," Grace continued, holding her hands up. "I'm not stealing artifacts, well not really. And I'm certainly not replacing them with replicas. That's terrible! I hope you would never think I'd do that."

"I didn't, Grace," said Derek soothingly.

"Well what *did* you do?" asked Sam, growing impatient.

"Okay," said Grace. "I did take a few small, worthless pieces of iron. Nothing that valuable, just some old tacks that we found in the ground."

"Why would you steal those if they're not worth much?" asked Sam. That didn't make any sense.

"We were melting them down into jewelry to have a keepsake from our experience at Jamestown. Like a memento."

"Jewelry?" asked Caitlin.

"Wait a minute," said Sam. "You said *we*. Who's *we*? Are you working with someone else?"

Grace's face blushed and she bit her bottom lip. "I'm not supposed to say anything."

"It's a little late for that," said Caitlin.

"Toby and I are in love," Grace proclaimed finally. "We're getting married. And we wanted to make wedding rings from metal that came out of the ground of Jamestown, since we both love history so much. We were going to use the kiln here at the Glasshouse to melt down the metal and then pour it into the molds for the rings."

"What!?" exclaimed Derek. His face fell like he was devastated.

Sam opened his mouth in surprise. "I did not see that coming."

"That's kind of romantic," said Caitlin, smiling.

Derek shook his head. "How *could* you, Grace?"

Grace tilted her head, clearly not understanding about Derek's silly crush on her. "I know, we shouldn't have taken the metal without asking. It was stupid. But I swear to you, I did not take the artifacts. It wasn't us! I don't know who did, but when I came down here this evening to turn on the unused pottery kiln, there was already something baking in it. The only people who have anything to do with the Glasshouse are Mariana and the other artisans, but I thought they focused on only glassware."

"Marcus!" said Derek.

Sam shrugged, his back to the Glasshouse. "Maybe, but remember we also thought it might be Patrick, he had the opportunity—" Sam stopped talking when he saw the look on Derek's and Caitlin's faces. He slowly turned around.

Standing behind him was Marcus with a sinister look on his face. In his hand was an iron-blowing rod. "You kids just couldn't leave it alone, could you?" he growled.

# CHAPTER TWENTY-FOUR

Sam's eyes opened wide.

"Marcus, what are you doing?" shrieked Grace.

"What I should have done before," Marcus answered. "You kids don't belong here. You're only getting in the way of the real science. It's a shame too, because now not only do you know about my expert pottery skills, Grace does too." He took a step toward them.

"I didn't see anything, really," said Grace nervously.

"Sure you didn't," mocked Marcus.

"It was *you* meeting someone out at the church that night, wasn't it?" said Caitlin.

"Oh, you saw that, did you?" said Marcus, shifting his attention to Caitlin. "Maybe you're more resourceful than I gave you credit for."

"What have you done, Marcus?" asked Grace heatedly. "Are you stealing the artifacts? How could you? I thought you believed in Jamestown."

"Jamestown!" Marcus cackled. "What is Jamestown, Grace? A bunch of holes in the ground? A four-hundred-year-old garbage site? It's just the foundations of buildings laid by colonists who killed and ate each other in desperation. It's not helping anyone. It's merely sad." He was waving the blow rod wildly through the air like a conductor's wand.

"We don't learn anything from this information we're digging up. We don't make our lives better, we just keep proving that we continue to make the same foolish mistakes." He took a step closer to them, an angry gleam in his eye. "So I decided to make it worth my while. If collectors on the black market want to pay big money for a crusty vase, then let them have it."

"That was my vase," muttered Sam.

Marcus narrowed his eyes. "That was *my* vase, boy," he snarled in a deep voice. "Do you know how many years I have toiled in that lab and others like it? Or how many years of schooling it took to train for this job? I've dedicated most of my life to this science, working to help others learn about the past. Do you know what it's gotten me? Nothing. There aren't riches in archeology for lab scientists, let me tell you. So why shouldn't I get my piece?"

"You're sick, Marcus," cried Grace. "You're a disgrace to Jamestown and all it stands for."

Sam shook his head. Marcus had gone crazy. They had to do something.

Marcus stuck his metal rod into the ground and looked around them in the woods. "All that talk about discovering America's beginnings? Well this is my part of the American way, taking what's coming to me."

Noticing that Marcus had turned his attention away from them, Derek nodded at Sam and pushed Marcus to the side. "Run!" he yelled.

With Marcus distracted, they all rushed into the Glasshouse. Sam turned around to see Marcus picking himself up off the path, his eyes ablaze.

"Hide!" said Derek, crouching behind one of the heavy tables near the kiln.

"This way!" called Grace, waving Sam and Caitlin into the gift shop. She pointed to a dark corner behind a shelf filled with glassware as she crouched out of sight behind the register counter.

"What are we going to do?" asked Caitlin as she huddled next to Sam in the shadows. "He's lost his mind."

"I don't know," said Sam. "Just hold still."

Marcus walked into the Glasshouse, his feet stepping heavily on the old wooden boards. Sam thought back to his meeting with Marcus in the lab. Marcus had yelled at him when he'd asked to take a picture, and he did seem super concerned about keeping his lab organized, but Sam never imagined he could act this way. Sam couldn't see Derek in the other room, but he hoped he was safe.

"You can't hide forever," Marcus bellowed, moving slowly through the kiln room. "None of this had anything to do with you, Grace. I had it all working perfectly until you started nosing around."

His voice paused near the kiln. Sam peered through the wide slits in the wooden wallboards. He saw Marcus moving a lever, then heard the giant kiln click on, the one they'd watched Mariana use to heat the glass into molten lava. It hissed loudly, sucking up the natural gas into flames, growing hotter and hotter. The open door of the oven cast an eerie orange glow out into the room. Its reflection danced and leapt against the rows of glass on the shelves where they were hiding, like a funhouse room of mirrors. It was like a hundred tiny flames darting all around them.

Sam caught his breath as Marcus pulled another of the long blowing rods from the furnace, this one glowing bright orange.

"Do you know how hot this kiln gets to melt the glass?" Marcus shouted as he walked toward them, holding the rod in front of him like a sword. "Two thousand degrees."

Sam gulped and Caitlin reached over and grabbed his

hand.

"The heat would kill you before you even entered the center of the kiln," Marcus continued. "Does that seem worth the trouble for some simple artifacts? No one seemed to notice my handiwork until that fool Patrick sent one of my pieces off to the Smithsonian for analysis. I'll admit that was unexpected. Without that, no one would have ever known."

I would have known, thought Sam, because I saw *my* vase too. He froze as Marcus entered the gift shop.

"I know you're in here," Marcus growled. He was stalking them like a tiger. "I'm not sure what you think you're going to accomplish by trying to get in my way. You and the professor think you can take credit for everything. Well you're not going to be the ones to bring down my career, not after all I've worked for."

He suddenly shouted out, slashing the glowing rod through the air like a sword. It smashed through a full shelf of glassware and then another. Shards of colored glass flew everywhere, raining down on the floor. Sam and Caitlin covered their heads with their hands under the spray of shattered glass.

Marcus leaned over the register counter and smiled. "Trapped like a rat," he cackled, reaching down and pulling Grace up by her arm.

"We have to do something," Caitlin whispered.

Sam felt frozen like a stone as they crouched behind

the shelf. He watched Marcus pull Grace closer to him, the burning rod only inches away from her face. He could hardly look.

"Why don't you pick on someone your own size, Marcus!" a voice shouted from the doorway. Derek slammed his body into Marcus, sending him smashing into a full case of glassware that stood against the wall.

"Ahh!" Marcus screamed, falling backwards as glass flew everywhere.

"Run, you guys!" Derek called. He reached down to help Grace up, but she'd caught a bit of the blow as well and she seemed dazed.

Sam and Caitlin jumped out of their hiding spot and ran across the glass-covered floor, broken glass crunching under their feet. They passed Marcus, who was slouched under a part of the shelf, blood dripping from his forehead. As soon as they were outside, they turned to see if Derek and Grace were behind them. Sam called out as somehow Marcus managed to reach out and grab the blow rod from the floor, striking it hard against Grace's shin as she tried to leave the room.

She screamed out in pain, falling to the glass-covered floor as Marcus pulled himself up and staggered forward.

"Consider that my engagement present," he jeered, moving past her toward Derek.

"Derek, come on!" called Sam, pausing with Caitlin just outside the exit. He'd didn't want to leave Grace, but they had to get out and call for help. Derek hesitated, looking at Grace on the ground, clutching her leg, even as Marcus lunged toward him.

She looked up and waved him on. "Go! I'm okay."

Derek turned and caught up with Sam and Caitlin. They ran out of the building and up the trail.

"What about Grace?" asked Caitlin.

"We need to draw him away from her," panted Derek. "That's the only way to help her right now."

Sam glanced back to see Marcus hobbling after them. He must have injured his leg when he crashed into the shelves of glass. They burst out of the path toward their bikes just as a Jeep skidded to a stop on the road.

"Help us!" cried Caitlin.

Toby leaped out of the driver's seat, running toward them. "Where's Grace?"

"Marcus has gone crazy," said Derek, pointing down the trail.

# CHAPTER TWENTY-FIVE

Toby bolted toward the Glasshouse as Marcus rounded the bend. He limped heavily, but still carried the metal rod in his hand. The blood from the gash in his head had smeared against his cheek like ugly makeup. Sam barely recognized the scientist he'd met in the lab.

"Where's Grace?" Toby yelled, moving toward Marcus.

"Get out of my way, Toby," snarled Marcus as another car pulled to a stop on the road behind them. The professor and Patrick jumped out and ran toward them.

"Not a chance," said Toby, straining to look down the path past where Marcus stood. "What have you done with her?"

"Marcus!" the professor shouted, hurrying past where

Sam, Caitlin, and Derek stood. "What are you doing to these children?" He turned to Patrick next to him. "Call the police."

Marcus grimaced as he wiped the blood from his face. "Oh, isn't this precious? The gang is all here, ready to bring me down. Everything in the name of history, right, Doc?"

"Whatever you've done isn't worth all this, Marcus," the professor answered, walking tentatively forward until he was side by side with Toby.

"Oh, no?" said Marcus, leaning up against a tree. "No one is bigger than the project, are they, Doc?" He seemed to be swaying. Sam wondered if he'd hurt himself even more seriously than his bleeding head let on.

A flash of metal came from behind, sending Marcus falling forward. He thudded to his knees, then onto the ground in a clump. Sam looked up to see Grace standing where Marcus had been, an iron blow rod in her hand. Marcus lay still on the ground in front of her, knocked unconscious.

"Have a seat," Grace muttered, as Toby rushed forward and she collapsed into his arms.

"Holy mackerel!" shouted Derek.

"Grace, are you okay?" said Caitlin, joining Toby by her side.

She nodded faintly, attempting a smile. "I don't think I'll be running any races for a while. He whacked my leg pretty good. But the rod wasn't hot enough to really do any damage."

The professor looked over at them in bewilderment. "What in the world has happened here? I got Derek's message and came as quickly as I could, but someone needs to start explaining things."

Sam looked over at his brother. "You called him?"

Derek nodded. "Quietly, while I was hiding. We couldn't just sit there, you know."

Sam was impressed. His brother had saved the day twice in just a few minutes. And he'd saved Grace too. Sam looked at the professor, hardly knowing where to begin. "We figured out that Marcus is the one who has been sending fake artifacts to the Smithsonian."

"I can't believe it," the professor bellowed.

"We thought it was Grace at first," added Caitlin.

"*You* thought it was Grace," said Derek defensively. He gave a silly grin to Grace. "I never doubted you."

Grace smiled. "Derek, thank you for pushing that shelf over on Marcus to save me. That was very brave." She leaned over and gently kissed his cheek. "Thank you."

For the first time Sam could remember, Derek was speechless. His entire face turned as red as a tomato. Sam burst out laughing.

Grace turned to the professor. "I do have a confession to make though, Doc."

"Oh?" said the professor. "I don't know if I can bear too many more revelations this evening."

"I did steal something from Jamestown."

"Actually, Doc, *we* stole something," said Toby, squeezing Grace's hand.

The professor raised his eyebrows. "Both of you?"

"Don't worry, it's not as bad as you think it is." Sam patted the professor on the back reassuringly.

"That's a matter of opinion," Derek grumbled.

"Toby and I took some iron tacks from the dig site," explained Grace.

"Iron tacks?" said the professor. "What in the world for?"

"We wanted to melt them down to make rings," said Toby eagerly. "Grace and I are getting married."

The professor's brow furrowed in confusion, then a wide smile filled his face. "Why that is tremendous news!" he exclaimed. "How have I not heard about this sooner?"

"We thought it might seem unprofessional," explained Toby.

"You're not mad?" asked Grace.

"Considering everything that has been going on today, Grace, a little bit of worthless iron is the least of my worries," the professor laughed.

"Congratulations, guys," said Patrick.

Just then a police car pulled to a stop at the top of the

road and two officers walked cautiously toward the group. "Everyone okay here?" the first one asked.

"I think so, Officer," said the professor. "But this man needs to be taken into custody, and he may need medical attention."

Grace explained to the officers what had happened at the Glasshouse and how Marcus had attacked them with the blow rod. He began to stir as the officers walked up. They pulled him to his feet, cuffing his hands behind his back.

Sam gave Marcus a worried look. "Are you okay?"

"Sam, don't ask him that!" said Derek.

Marcus moaned and tried to get his bearings. The professor walked over to him, but only shook his head silently.

"Don't look at me like that, Doc," Marcus hissed. "You know history well enough to know that most things don't have a storybook ending."

"Sadly, you're right, Marcus," the professor replied. "But this could have been avoided. You knew better."

"All right, let's get down to the station. We can sort this out there," said one of the officers.

# CHAPTER TWENTY-SIX

Their parents came early the next morning. It was all that Derek could do to talk their mom out of driving over the night before when he had called to share what had happened at the Glasshouse. Even though Sam knew they hadn't done anything wrong, his parents knew he and Derek had a knack for getting into trouble. And they did worry. Sam preferred to think they had a knack for solving mysteries, but he supposed it was a matter of perspective.

"What's the matter?" he asked Derek as they finished packing up their clothes and sleeping bags in the dorm room. "You're not still thinking about Grace, are you?"

"Maybe," said Derek glumly.

Sam tried not to laugh. He wasn't sure how Derek had gotten such a big crush on someone so much older than him in the first place, but it was pretty funny. "At least she didn't turn out to be a criminal."

"I know."

"And Toby's a great guy, don't you think?"

"Yeah," said Derek, shrugging. "It's just a lot to take in."

"Well, I'll agree with that," said Sam. "I can't believe Marcus turned out to be so crazy."

Derek laughed. "He was like that mad scientist in the movies, what was his name?"

"Dr. Jekyll and Mr. Hyde?"

"Yeah, that one. It just goes to show you never can tell."

Sam's phone buzzed. It was a text from Caitlin.

*I'm outside, come down*

"Let's go," said Sam, hauling his bag to the door.

"There they are!" exclaimed their mom, who was standing next to the steps with Dad, Caitlin, and her parents. She smothered them both in a big hug.

"Another quiet week at camp, huh, boys?" said Dad, his eyebrows raised suspiciously.

"You know how it is, Dad," said Derek, grinning.

"I do," Dad answered. "That's what always worries me."

Sam smiled as he saw Toby, Grace, and Professor Evanshade walking toward them. The professor had said he wanted to speak to their parents before they left. Sam was happy to have another grown-up explain the situation.

"Hello, everyone!" the professor greeted them.

"Hey, Doc," answered Derek.

"Thank you so much for calling," Mom said to the professor. Sam's eyes widened with surprise. He hadn't known the professor had called Mom and Dad directly, although it made sense that he would.

"It's not a problem at all," said the professor. "Once again, I need to be thanking you and my young friends here."

Sam grinned up at his parents. It felt good to have the professor back up their story. Mom and Dad trusted him.

"That's good to hear," answered Mr. Murphy, his arm around Caitlin's shoulder. Sam was pretty sure he and Derek were on Mr. Murphy's good side, since he'd been part of their adventure up in the Blue Ridge Mountains at Swannanoa, but he was still pretty protective of Caitlin.

"Your kids did a great job this week," said Toby.

Grace gave Derek a wink, and Sam thought he noticed his brother's face reddening once more.

"Did you learn anything more about how Marcus was switching out the artifacts?" asked Caitlin.

"Yes, I think we've gotten to the bottom of most of it," said the professor. "It seems that Marcus had a contact he was meeting with secretly. The contact would take the real items that had been uncovered and sell them, while Marcus would make a fake to take its place. The authorities are still working on tracking this man down, but Marcus has provided a name, so it should just be a matter of time."

"I knew it," said Derek. "That was him we saw in the shadows of the old church that night."

The professor nodded. "I wish you would have told me about that right away, kids. Keeping that kind of information to yourselves made this situation much more dangerous."

Sam gave Derek an I-told-you-so glance.

"We've been working on that with them, Professor," said Mom.

Professor Evanshade chuckled. "No doubt. Well, thank goodness it wasn't any worse than it was. Your injuries notwithstanding, of course, Grace."

"I think I'll be okay, Doc," answered Grace. "It's just bruised."

"Oh, and guess what?" Caitlin exclaimed, turning to her parents. "Grace and Toby are getting married!"

"Well, congratulations," Mrs. Murphy responded.

"Thanks," Grace said. "Doc's letting us work with Mariana to mold our rings in the kiln. It will be our own special memory from Jamestown."

"Another secret that might have been communicated better, I guess," admitted Toby.

"So Marcus made the reproductions down at the Glasshouse in the kiln?" asked Sam.

"Apparently it was a hidden talent of his," answered the professor. "He was able to use his extensive knowledge of the period to recreate the items flawlessly."

"Until they were analyzed at the Smithsonian, that is," added Toby.

"Yes, that seems to be the one thing Marcus didn't anticipate," said the professor. "Patrick sent one of the reproductions to the Smithsonian, and of course it failed their analysis."

"There was one more thing he didn't anticipate," said Sam.

"What's that, Sam?" asked the professor.

"Us!"

Everyone laughed, releasing some of the tension that had been building up for a long time.

Sam pulled out his phone and showed the picture of his vase to the professor. He apologized for breaking the rules, but the professor seemed to be happy for one more piece of evidence that proved items had been tampered with. "I'm headed back up to Washington tomorrow to get things straightened out. Needless to say, it should be a much easier discussion than my last trip."

"Speaking of trips," said Dad, "I think it's time for us to head back home."

"I'm sorry that this week of Field School didn't work

out exactly as you'd planned," said the professor, "but I'm glad you kids were here."

"Thanks for inviting us," said Caitlin.

"I will definitely not forget it," said Derek.

The professor smiled. "I've said this to the three of you before, but I'll say it once more. I have a feeling we will be crossing paths again."

"You guys could make some great archaeologists someday," said Toby.

"Thanks," said Derek. He waved at Grace. "Good luck uncovering more history."

As they followed their parents to the parking lot along the brick sidewalk, the historic college buildings all around them, Sam wondered if they hadn't already started making their own history. Uncovering history was a lot like solving a mystery. You never knew where the twists and turns would lead you. Or when one small step could reveal something spectacular. He couldn't wait to see what would come next!

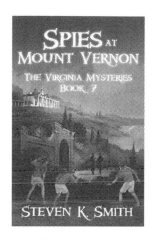

Sam, Derek, and Caitlin love solving mysteries, and when they
visit Washington, DC, spies are lurking. What starts out as a
fun game of pretend on the National Mall turns all too real
when they follow a mysterious man to a meeting deep within
the Capitol. To keep government secrets from falling into the
wrong hands, the kids must work with federal agents and
travel to historic Mount Vernon for a state dinner with the
president and his son. Dead drops, cyphers and spy chases are
all part of what might be their most dangerous adventure ever
—if it isn't their last.

# ACKNOWLEDGMENTS

The more that I learned about Jamestown and its key role in America's beginnings, I knew it needed to be part of the series. As is often the case, the hardest part was narrowing down which aspects to include in the story. I work hard to make the facts in my stories as accurate as possible, but there is usually a fictional mystery line. In this book, while there have been countless discoveries in and around the original Jamestown Fort, to my knowledge there is no "West Wall," and the curators of the scientific laboratory are quite honest and trustworthy. The Glasshouse is really a cool place to visit, but they do not also spin pottery there. Or do they…

As in previous books, Dr. Evanshade fills in nicely for the real-life scientists and historians. At Jamestown, I enjoyed meeting with David Givens, Sr. Staff Archaeologist for the Jamestown Rediscovery team, who shared some perspectives about the preservation process on the island. If you haven't been on the island to witness the amazing work from the past twenty years of David and all of Dr. William Kelso's team, I highly recommend it.

Many thanks are due to others who helped make this book possible. Kim Sheard, Lana Krumwiede, LeslieJean Anderson, and Polgarus Studio aided with editing and proofreading, covering my many mistakes. Dane from ebooklaunch.com designs all my covers, which continue to garner rave reviews. Special thanks to Julie Tate and Hanover County Public Schools, Jill Stefanovich, Mary Patterson, Anita Fluker, Sandra Koch, Jodi Bailey, Rhonda Riddick, Theresa Harris, and Christy Martin for going above and beyond to help get my books in the hands of young readers.

I am so blessed to have the support of my family— Mary, for her patience with my jumping feetfirst into my sometimes crazy dreams; Matthew, Josh, and Aaron for handling the extra attention and questions at school even when they might not feel like it; and Mom, Dad, Alicia, Ryan, Ray, Jean, Robin and Julia for your love and support. It is so appreciated.

Finally, thank you to all my readers who have made this possible. Your enthusiasm, smiles, questions and feedback have helped more than you know. I am so excited about what 2018 will bring!

# ABOUT THE AUTHOR

Steven K. Smith is the author of *The Virginia Mysteries*, *Brother Wars*, and *Final Kingdom* series for middle grade readers. He lives with his wife, three sons, and a golden retriever in Richmond, Virginia.

For more information, visit:

www.stevenksmith.net

steve@myboys3.com

## DID YOU ENJOY SHADOWS AT JAMESTOWN?
### WOULD YOU ... REVIEW?

Online reviews are crucial for indie authors like me. They help bring credibility and make books more discoverable by new readers. No matter where you purchased your book, if you could take a few moments and give an honest review at one of the following websites, I'd be so grateful.

*Amazon.com*
*BarnesandNoble.com*
*Goodreads.com*

Thank you and thanks for reading!

Steve

Made in the USA
Coppell, TX
10 May 2021